P9-BXW-697

THE HORSESHOE TRILOGIES

Charity at Home

Read all the books in the first
Horseshoe Trilogy:

Book #1: Keeping Faith
Book #2: Last Hope
Book #3: Sweet Charity

And in the second Horseshoe Trilogy:

Book #4: In Good Faith
Book #5: Where There's Hope
Book #6: Charity at Home

COMING SOON:

Book #7: Leap of Faith

THE HORSESHOE TRILOGIES

Charity at Home

by
Lucy Daniels

Wilton Public Library
PO Box 447
Wilton, IA 52778

(563) 732-2583

HYPERION
New York

Special thanks to Susannah Leigh

If you purchased this book without a cover, you should be aware that this book is stolen property. It was reported as "unsold and destroyed" to the publisher, and neither the author nor the publisher has received any payment for this "stripped" book.

Text copyright © 2003 by Working Partners Limited
Cover illustration copyright © 2003 by Tristan Elwell

The Horseshoe Trilogies and the Volo colophon are trademarks of Disney Enterprises, Inc. Volo® is a registered trademark of Disney Enterprises, Inc.

All rights reserved. No part of this book may be reproduced in any form or by any means, electronic or mechanical, including photocopying, recording, or by any information storage and retrieval system, without written permission from the publisher. For information address Volo, 114 Fifth Avenue, New York, New York 10011-5690.

Printed in the United States of America

First U.S. edition, 2003
1 3 5 7 9 10 8 6 4 2

This book is set in 12.5-point Life Roman.
ISBN 0-7868-1749-6

Visit www.volobooks.com

For Daisy, hoping you find your own perfect pony

CHAPTER ONE

Josie Grace opened the car door and stepped out onto the driveway in front of her house.

As she turned to wave good-bye to her friend Anna Marshall and her twin brother, Ben Marshall, Josie heard the roar of an engine behind her. She looked around to see a large white van pulling into the driveway next to her house. HADWELLS MOVERS was written on the side in curly gold letters. Four men jumped out and began unloading heavy-looking, big boxes from the back of the van.

Anna's mother, Lynne, rolled down the car window. "It looks like you've got new neighbors," she observed.

"They must be moving into Dove House. That's the big farmhouse behind Charity's field. It's been empty since we moved here."

Anna leaned forward and stuck her head out of the window for a closer look. "Maybe it's someone tall, dark, and handsome," she said mysteriously, her brown eyes shining.

"Yeah, with four legs, a mane, and a tail," Ben finished.

Josie laughed. "Now that sounds more like it."

"Very funny, Ben." Anna nudged her brother in the ribs.

Ben rolled his eyes and ran a hand through his curly black hair. Quieter than his twin, he was used to her good-natured teasing.

Josie watched as the movers struggled to unload a large chest from the back of the van. It looked like hard work on such a beautiful summer's day. She was glad she wasn't moving again. Josie and her parents had recently moved to a new house. When they had moved away from School Farm, the place where Josie had spent the first twelve years of her life, she had never dreamed they would find somewhere to live as nice as this house. When her dad had found the house with a yard big enough for her horse, Charity, Josie was very happy. It had still been hard to give up two of the school horses, Hope and Faith, but Josie had found them homes nearby. Anna and Ben didn't live too far away, but now they and Josie needed their moms to drive them to each other's house. But, as Anna pointed out, they'd been best friends for three years. They weren't going to let a little obstacle like that get in their way.

Josie turned to her friends again. "Good-bye, everybody," she said. "Thanks for the ride."

"It was nice to see you, Josie," Lynne Marshall replied. "Say hello to your mother for me. Tell her I'll drop in for a visit soon. I've been so busy organizing the art exhibition for the festival, I haven't had time to think about anything else." Lynne worked as an art therapist at Friendship House, a home for children with special needs. They were holding a festival for all the children and parents, and Lynne was planning to display some of the children's artwork.

"I will," Josie promised. "And don't forget, Anna." She turned to her friend. "You're coming for a sleepover next week."

Anna grinned back at her. "You bet," she said.

"You two will end up spending the whole summer vacation at each other's house," Lynne commented.

"Of course," Josie replied, tucking an unruly strand of wavy, dark auburn hair behind her ear. "When we're not riding Charity."

"You and your horse!" Lynne said, smiling. She waved good-bye and turned the car back down Josie's driveway.

Josie opened the front door of her house and let her bag fall onto the tiled floor of the little entrance hall. "Hi, Mom, I'm home," she called, walking through the house to find her mother.

"In here," Mary Grace called back.

Josie found her mom seated at the dining room table. There was a pile of paperwork in front of her.

"Bills!" her mother exclaimed. "Wherever you go, they always find you." She smiled up at Josie. "So, did you have a good time at Anna's?"

"Great, thanks." Josie sat down at the table opposite her mother. "Lynne says hello. She says she'll come by and see you soon." Josie's mother and Lynne Marshall were almost as close as Josie and Anna.

"I'd like that. It seems like I haven't seen Lynne for ages." Mary Grace pushed the paperwork aside and leaned back in her chair. "Oh, before I forget, Jill Atterbury called. She wanted to know if you'd like to bring Charity over to see Faith some time soon. She was hoping you two could go riding."

"That's a great idea," Josie said happily. "Charity always likes seeing Faith."

Faith was Mary Grace's first horse. It had been hard to give her up, but the Atterburys' was the perfect home for Faith. Jill Atterbury was exactly the same age as Josie. She had suffered terrible injuries in a car accident, and she had only recently started riding again. Steady, loyal Faith had turned out to be the ideal horse for her.

"Did you see the movers?" Mrs. Grace asked.

"You couldn't miss them!" Josie answered. "The van was practically taking up the whole road."

Basil, the family's little brown terrier, scrambled up from his basket by the window and rushed over to greet her. Josie bent down to scratch him under the chin, and Basil wagged his tail enthusiastically.

"Well, I don't know much," Mrs. Grace said. "I think it's a family. I saw a little girl running around

5

in the garden. All those boxes. I have to admit, I feel for them—moving is hard work." Suddenly she looked thoughtful. Josie knew that her mother wasn't just thinking about the packing. Moving from School Farm had been hard on everyone. Leaving the stables had meant that Mary Grace had given up teaching people to ride, something she loved passionately.

"It's hard to say good-bye, isn't it?" Josie said sympathetically. "They must be feeling pretty strange, especially the little girl."

"I would imagine." Mrs. Grace put her arm around Josie and gave her a warm hug. "We should go and welcome them once they've moved in."

Josie fished out some tea bags from the jar on the counter and popped them into the waiting pot. "We could take something to cheer them up, too," she suggested.

"That's a good idea." Mrs. Grace thought for a minute. "Why don't we bake them a cake?"

"Did someone mention baking?" Robert Grace, Josie's dad, said as he came in through the back door. "Look, the chickens have laid," he added, walking over to get a bowl from the counter. "These are the first eggs since we moved here. The chickens must be starting to feel at home."

"Josie and I were thinking of baking a cake for the neighbors," Mrs. Grace explained. "The ones who just moved in next door."

"Excellent idea. Baking is my specialty." Mr. Grace placed the eggs gently in the bowl. He walked over to the shelf of cookbooks and began to flip through them. "Now, let me see," he muttered to himself. "Somewhere I've got a great recipe for chocolate chestnut meringue flan. Or there's the plum and apricot . . ."

Mr. Grace was an excellent, and sometimes adventurous, cook. Mrs. Grace was more cautious, though. "Now's not the time to try out some complicated recipe. Why don't you play it safe with brownies? We don't want to scare the new people off."

"Brownies? Hmm . . . good suggestion," Mr. Grace nodded. "In fact I have a special double-chocolate brownie recipe."

"Double-chocolate brownies? My favorite," Josie announced. "The best part is licking the bowl!"

Mr. Grace smiled at her. "Do you want to help me make them?" he suggested.

"Yum, yes, please," Josie said quickly.

"I'll look for the recipe. Let's plan on making them tomorrow," said Mr. Grace. "I'll make sure we have all the ingredients."

Josie made her way to the back door. "Sounds good. I need to go check on Charity," she said. "Count me in on those brownies, Dad."

The sun was just beginning to set as Josie walked to the fence that bordered the lawn and Charity's field. She could see her horse standing by the gate. The light was behind Charity and it made her gray coat shine like silver. Charity was standing so quietly that for a moment she looked like a marble statue. Josie's heart skipped a beat. She still couldn't quite believe that Charity was hers to keep forever. Best of all, she lived right here, so Josie only had to step out of the back door, or look out of her bedroom window, to see her. Bringing Charity with her from School Farm had made Josie's move a lot easier.

Josie unlatched the gate and closed it carefully behind her. She reached up to put her arms around the horse.

"Hello," she said, scratching Charity behind her ear. Charity dropped her soft pink muzzle to sniff around in Josie's pockets.

"Hey, cut it out," Josie said, laughing. "You just want a treat, don't ya? Lucky for you I've come prepared."

Josie reached into the pocket of her jeans and fished out some baby carrots. Charity crunched contentedly while Josie went over to her stall to grab the brush box.

"I'll just give you a quick brush and then you'll get your real dinner."

Josie brushed dust from Charity's coat with methodical strokes while the horse stood still, enjoying the attention. Except for the sound of the brush, everything was quiet and peaceful. Josie let her thoughts wander, imagining the long summer vacation stretching before her. Time spent with Charity and glorious days of riding lay ahead. As Josie moved around to comb out Charity's tail, a slight movement in the hedge behind her caught her eye. For a split second, Josie had a strange feeling they were not alone. Charity sensed it too. She lifted her head and sniffed the air.

Josie felt her heart quicken slightly. "Hello?" she called out cautiously. "Anyone there?"

Silence.

Josie stood looking around for a moment. She strained her ears but she couldn't hear anything else. She shrugged and turned back to Charity. "Well, you're just about finished," she said loudly, trying to sound braver than she felt. "Just don't go rolling in the dirt again the minute my back's turned."

Josie kissed Charity on the nose and turned to put the brush away. Suddenly, there it was again, the slight movement in the hedges. This time, Josie was sure she could hear breathing too. "Did you hear that, Charity?" she whispered to her horse. It seemed that Charity had, for she began walking over toward the hedge to investigate. Josie followed the horse, calling as she went. "Hello? Anyone there?"

Josie and Charity reached the hedge. Charity sniffed around in the roots of the bushes and Josie peered over the top, her heart pounding. The hedge separated Dove House from her house. Josie looked over and saw the neighbors' lawn and house in the distance. Around the corner she could just make out a stream running along the bottom of the lawn where it sloped away from the house. Suddenly, a flash of brown fur caught her eye as a rabbit darted out from beneath the bushes, rustling the leaves as it went. Josie put her hand to her mouth and laughed with relief to see it scampering away. "You scared me, bunny," she said, shaking her head.

Everything was still now, and the garden looked empty. Charity had lost interest in the rabbit, finding some tasty grass to munch instead. Josie scanned the hedges one last time, then she glanced at the lengthening shadows on the grass and patted her horse on the neck. "Come on, Charity," she said. "Let's get you some dinner."

CHAPTER TWO

The next morning, Josie rode Charity over to visit Jill and Faith. The girls had spoken on the phone the night before and had decided to take Faith and Charity out for a nice long and relaxed ride.

Josie turned Charity off the road and up Jill's driveway. She rode Charity right up to the front door, sprang lightly down from the saddle, and rang the bell. Jill opened the door almost immediately.

"Are you ready?" Josie grinned at her.

"Of course," Jill said, laughing. "How funny to see a horse at the door. Come on. I'll go and open the gate to Faith's field. I'm sure she'll be happy to see Charity. I think Faith needs some exercise. She's feeling pretty frisky today."

"Charity's pretty excited, too," Josie said. As if in reply, Charity stamped at the ground impatiently with one front hoof.

Faith was standing in the middle of her field, but when she saw Josie leading Charity toward her, the bay horse trotted over immediately, whinnying excitedly. Charity pulled at the reins and Josie had to jog to keep up with her.

"I'd call that a warm welcome," Jill said with a smile, as Faith reached her head over the gate to nuzzle Charity's nose with her lips. Charity stood still, enjoying all the attention from the gentle old horse.

"Should we tack Faith up?" Josie asked. "Charity's definitely ready for a ride."

"So am I," Jill replied. "I'll just go and get Faith's tack. Would you mind giving me a hand with the saddle?" To lessen the pressure on her injured back and hip, Jill had learned to ride sidesaddle. The sidesaddle was much heavier than a regular saddle.

"Sure," agreed Josie. She followed Jill to the stable where the tack was kept and helped her to lift the sidesaddle down from its peg. "All right, I've got the back," Josie said, slipping her hand underneath the leather. With her free hand she grabbed the bridle from its hook and, together, the two girls carried the tack back to the field. Faith stood patiently as Josie helped Jill lift the saddle onto the horse's back.

Jill gave Faith a pat. "Oh, good old Faith, she never complains, even though the saddle's so heavy."

"It makes you look so classy." Josie slipped the bridle over Faith's nose. "And I think that once you're on Faith's back, the weight sort of gets spread out—so it's not bad for her at all."

"I suppose not," Jill agreed. "It did feel strange at first, though. For both of us." She pulled herself up into the saddle and swung her legs over Faith's neck.

"I remember," Josie replied, thinking back to the first time Jill had tried out the saddle. "But Faith's so patient and you didn't give up, that was the main thing. And now you look really comfortable up there."

"I think Faith and I are both used to it now," Jill responded. "To tell you the truth, I wouldn't mind if I was sitting upside down and back to front, as long as it meant I could still ride."

"No circus tricks today, please, Jill." Mrs. Atterbury said, laughing, as she came to see the girls off. "Now where are you planning to go?" she asked.

Jill thought for a moment. "We'll go along the road to the big field and then follow the stream back."

"Don't stay out more than an hour," her mother warned. "I don't want you to tire yourself out."

"I won't," Jill promised, and the two girls turned their horses down the driveway, waving good-bye to Mrs. Atterbury as they went.

Josie and Jill walked the horses to the edge of the field and through the gate. It was a perfect summer morning. Small white clouds trailed across the blue sky like wisps of smoke and bees buzzed lazily in the still air. Josie turned Charity off the gravel path and on to the edge of a field, golden with wheat. Jill followed close behind. There was nothing like the feeling of riding a horse cross-country on a warm summer's day. Josie took a deep breath of fresh air and happily patted Charity's neck.

"It's days like these that make all the hard work worth it," Jill sighed, echoing Josie's thoughts. "All those boring back-strengthening exercises have meant I can ride like this again."

"You've been so good about doing your exercises," Josie agreed.

"Stubborn and single-minded, my dad calls it," said Jill, laughing. "Still, if you want something badly enough, you have to keep at it. And right now I want to canter. So does Faith."

Josie laughed. "I don't think Charity needs much encouragement. Come on." And with a thud of hooves they were off, cantering along the path at the edge of the field, Josie's auburn hair and Jill's blond hair flying out behind them. They came to a thundering halt at the top of the field where the grass met the trees.

"Fantastic!" Jill exclaimed, her eyes shining. "Faith almost caught up with Charity there."

"Not bad for an old lady," Josie said with a laugh.

They walked the horses peacefully through the quiet wood. Now that they had worked off some energy, both Charity and Faith seemed happy to ease the pace. They came out by the stream at the bottom of the wood. Faith walked a bit behind Charity. Sweat glistened on her broad bay flanks. As they followed the path along the stream, Faith stumbled on some loose earth. Her knees buckled briefly and her hooves slipped on the wet bank. Jill was thrown forward, but she managed to hang on. Josie didn't even have to halt Charity. The horse had stopped as soon as she heard Faith stumble. Josie turned around in the saddle to look back at Jill. "Are you all right?" she asked anxiously.

"Yes," Jill replied, a little breathless. "We're fine. Faith must have just tripped. I think she's probably getting tired."

Josie looked over at the older horse with a touch of concern. "Let's stop for a minute. Maybe the horses want something to drink," she suggested.

The girls dismounted and led their horses to the edge of the stream. As Charity and Faith bent their heads to drink, Josie felt the sun on her face and looked down at the silvery water.

"That looks so refreshing," she said. "Why don't we take our boots off and wade?"

"Good idea," Jill agreed quickly and, before Josie knew it, Jill had taken her boots and socks off and was standing ankle deep in the stream. "It's great," she called to Josie. "Come on, what are you waiting for?"

"Absolutely nothing." Josie laughed, peeling off her boots and socks and pulling up her jodhpurs as far as they would go. She dipped a toe in the water. "It's freezing!" she exclaimed.

"It's fine once you're in," Jill assured her.

Suddenly Josie felt a gentle push from behind, and she fell forward into the stream with a splash. Charity had pushed Josie in! Jill roared with laughter and Charity gave a triumphant little snort.

"You're right," Josie admitted, grinning. "It's not so bad once you're in. Thanks a lot, Charity."

After they had all cooled off, Josie and Jill dried their toes in the sunshine. After a while, they mounted the horses again and turned back toward home. As they emerged from the woods, Josie spotted a low tree trunk lying in the middle of the field. She turned to Jill. "That looks tempting," she said. "It's the perfect height to jump. You up for it?"

Jill hesitated for a moment, sizing up the log. Then she nodded her head and smiled. "I've been jumping a little bit with Sally over at Lonsdale," she told Josie, referring to the stable that both she, Anna, and Ben rode at. "We've jumped a bit higher than that, so I say, let's go for it."

"Are you sure?" Josie asked her. She didn't want Jill to feel any pressure.

"Positive," Jill replied firmly. "Why don't you go first, and Faith and I will follow."

"Good idea," Josie said and turned Charity toward the log. After her rest in the woods, Charity was ready to go. The lightest touch was all that it took to send her into a canter. They approached the jump squarely, and Charity popped neatly over it. Josie brought her to a halt and turned to watch Jill, who wasn't far behind.

Faith flew over the jump and landed safely on the other side. "Well done, Faith," Jill said breathlessly. She looked at Josie. "If you'd told me a year ago I'd be jumping, I wouldn't have believed it. But I'm so used to this sidesaddle now, and Faith is so steady, she gives me loads of confidence."

"You've made amazing progress," Josie agreed proudly. "And that goes for both of you."

Jill grinned at her and patted Faith's neck. "I think that was the perfect end to this ride," she exclaimed.

Josie nodded her head. "It's been great," she said. "But let's get these horses back in one piece."

"Okay," Jill said with a sigh.

* * *

"That was exactly an hour," Josie announced, checking her watch as they approached Faith's field. She turned to Jill. "How are you feeling?"

"Great!" Jill said and smiled. "But I think Faith's glad to be home." Jill unhooked her leg from the saddle and dismounted skillfully. "Why don't we give the horses a rubdown and then have some lemonade?" she suggested.

"Sounds like a good idea," Josie agreed. "I'll turn Charity out into Faith's field for a bit and give her a rest before I ride home."

A while later Josie peacefully rode Charity home, enjoying the quiet of the country and the warmth on her back. When she got home, she untacked the horse slowly and then turned her out into the field before heading back up the path to the house. As she opened the back door to the kitchen, Anna jumped out at her.

"Surprise!" she cried, her dark eyes shining.

"Anna! You scared me half to death!" Josie said, a smile tugging at her lips despite her efforts to frown.

Anna nodded in the direction of the dining room.

"Our moms are having coffee," she explained. "I practically begged Mom to come. Ben's playing tennis, and I'm super bored. And," she said turning in the direction of Mr. Grace, who was busy in the kitchen, "your Dad is about to make double-chocolate brownies and he said I could lick the bowl. How's that for perfect timing?" she said.

"Dad! You promised *me* that job!" Josie protested jokingly.

Mr. Grace turned around, his arms full of bowls. "You can both lick the bowls," he said, "but only if you help me make the brownies. Now I suggest a batch for us and a batch for the new neighbors."

Josie and Anna looked at each other and grinned. "That sounds like a plan," said Josie. "Let me just go wash my hands. I've been out riding. Oh, Anna," she said, turning to her friend. "I just had the best ride with Jill. We even jumped a fallen tree trunk! She's making so much progress with that sidesaddle."

"Good for her," Anna said. "And she really loves Faith, doesn't she?"

"Uh-huh." Josie nodded.

Mr. Grace placed a bag of flour on the counter in front of them. "I suggest we double the ingredients and then divide the brownies at the end. So that's eight cups of flour you need to measure and sift, please."

Josie thought for a moment. "If we're making double-chocolate brownies, doesn't that mean we need to quadruple the chocolate for two batches?" she asked slowly.

"It does indeed," Mr. Grace said. "I'm just going to melt it in this big saucepan."

Josie and Anna looked at each other and then at the flour. "Hang on a minute, Dad," Josie began.

"I think you might have given us the wrong job, Mr. Grace," Anna finished as both girls rushed over to the pan.

Mr. Grace looked confused.

"We'll melt the chocolate and you can weigh the flour," announced Josie. "Surely quadruple chocolate needs four hands? You've only got two."

Mr. Grace laughed. "You've got me on that one. But be careful. The water's hot. Oh, and—" He turned to stare at Anna, who was holding her spoon dangerously close to the melting chocolate. "No tasting yet!" he finished sternly.

"Sorry," said Anna quickly.

The three cooks stirred and mixed and measured. Even the dog, Basil, joined in, sniffing hopefully around their feet. As they poured the brownie mixture into the pans, Josie caught sight of Anna and laughed. "You've got chocolate all over your nose," she said.

"That must have been where I scratched it," Anna explained. "Well, look who's talking, Josie! You've got some in your hair."

Mr. Grace came over. "And you haven't even started licking the bowls!" He laughed. "Here you go, one for each of you."

"Yum!" Anna exclaimed. "You won't need to wash these bowls, Mr. Grace."

Thirty minutes later, the delicious smell of freshly baked brownies wafted out of the kitchen. Mr. Grace took the pan out of the oven and put it on the counter to cool. Josie inhaled their mouthwatering aroma as Mrs. Grace walked into the kitchen, followed by Anna's mom.

"Look at the two of you," Mrs. Grace exclaimed, laughing. "You're covered in chocolate." Basil rushed up to greet her. Mrs. Grace looked down at him and sighed. "Even Basil's got chocolate on him," she pointed out. "You must have been having fun."

"You could say that," Josie and Anna said at the same time.

"Well, something certainly smells delicious," said Lynne, sniffing the air.

"Chocolate brownies," Mr. Grace told her, wiping his hands on a dishrag. Then he smiled proudly. "Actually, they're *double*-chocolate brownies," he declared. "My new specialty!" He collapsed into a chair. "Now that I've finished cooking, I need a rest!" He sighed dramatically.

Josie laughed. "You know, Dad, sometimes I think being a drama teacher goes straight to your head." Mr. Grace had recently been made head of the English and drama departments at the high school.

Mrs. Grace turned to Lynne. "I'm just glad he made double-chocolate brownies. He was thinking of trying out a new recipe," she explained.

"Mexican chili chocolate cake," Mr. Grace said wistfully. "A culinary masterpiece."

"Masterpiece it may be," said Mrs. Grace. "But I wanted to give our new neighbors a warm welcome, not a chili welcome!"

Josie rolled her eyes and put her arm around her father. "Never mind, Dad," she told him. "You can save that one for the midnight feast Anna and I are going to have next week."

"Mmm, sounds good to me," Anna agreed, licking her lips.

Lynne Marshall laughed. "Well in that case, I'd better get you home so you can come back again." She turned to Mrs. Grace. "It was great catching up with you, Mary."

"You too, Lynne." Mrs. Grace smiled. "I'll walk you to the door."

"Bye, Josie," Anna called. "See you next week. And I'm looking forward to that chili chocolate cake, Mr. Grace," she added.

"Here," Josie said, wrapping some brownies up in aluminum foil. "Take some of these home. Careful, they're still a bit warm."

"Thanks," Anna said, clutching the package. "See you later."

"I think we'd better take the rest over to Dove House before they disappear," Mrs. Grace commented as Basil padded over and gazed longingly at the tin with wistful eyes.

"Can I come with you?" asked Josie. "I want to meet the neighbors, too, and I'll tell you all about my morning with Jill."

"I'd love to hear about it," Mrs. Grace said, smiling. "Want to get going?"

Mr. Grace carried the pans over to the sink. "Go ahead," he told her. "We've almost finished here, anyway. I can do the rest."

Basil gave a pleading whimper as he saw Mrs. Grace carrying the pan of brownies off.

"Never mind, Basil," whispered Josie, bending down to scratch the little dog under the chin. "I'll ask our new neighbors to save you the crumbs."

CHAPTER
THREE

Josie opened the back door for her mom, who was carrying the brownies. Together they headed along the back way to the neighbor's house. As they walked, Josie told her mother all about her morning with Jill and Faith.

"It was great to see Charity and Faith together, Mom," Josie said. "They looked so happy standing in the field after our ride."

"It is lucky that we've been able to keep in touch since our old horses are nearby," Mrs. Grace agreed. "I knew they'd all find the right homes eventually. Faith is perfect for Jill, and dear Hope loves Friendship House."

Charity's mother, Hope, had gone to live at Friendship House, a place where children with disabilities went for a type of vacation. The children at Friendship House loved the sweet-natured gray mare. Better still, because Lynne Marshall worked there, it meant that she was usually able to take Josie and Anna to visit Hope whenever they wanted.

"And this is definitely the best home for Charity," Josie agreed, stopping on the path to give Charity a pat as the horse poked her head over the fence. "Sorry, Charity, these brownies aren't for you," she added apologetically as the gray horse sniffed hopefully at the pan of treats.

"First Basil, and now Charity, too," Mrs. Grace said with a smile. "You would think we didn't feed our animals."

As the pair approached the house, they saw a slim dark-haired woman hanging out some laundry in the front yard. She didn't notice Josie and Mrs. Grace at first, but a small Jack Russell puppy leaped up at them, barking excitedly.

"Barker, shush," the woman called, turning to see

Mrs. Grace and Josie standing at the gate. "Hello," she said and smiled at them. "I hope the puppy didn't startle you. He's very friendly."

"He's adorable," said Josie, crouching down to pat the little puppy through the bars of the gate. "I can see why you call him Barker."

"That was my daughter Ellie's choice," the woman explained, putting down the laundry basket and walking over to them.

"I'm Mary Grace." Mrs. Grace held out her hand in welcome. "And this is my daughter, Josie. We live next door," Mrs. Grace pointed back along the path. "We brought you some chocolate brownies as a welcome to the neighborhood," she said.

"What a nice thought." The woman gratefully took the pan and opened the lid, peeping at the brownies. "Mmm, they smell delicious. We haven't had time to shop for food, so we've been living off grilled cheese and apples for the last few days. My husband's just gone to the supermarket now." She opened the gate. "Come in," she offered. "I'm Jenny Carter, and you've already met Barker." She smiled down at the little puppy who was pawing at her heels, anxious for brownie crumbs.

"Another brownie lover." Mrs. Grace laughed.

Josie's attention wandered as the grown-ups began chatting. She looked up at the big house, noticing how the ivy clambered its way over the gray stone. Like Sleeping Beauty's castle, Josie thought to herself. The driveway opened out into a courtyard area to the left of the house. Suddenly, Josie noticed what looked like two run-down stables, tucked away in the corner of the yard. Stables! Maybe the Carters were thinking of keeping horses. Josie decided then and there that her new neighbors looked very promising.

Beyond the courtyard and the house was a large backyard. Josie could just make out the stream at the very bottom, the sunlight reflecting off the water and making it sparkle. It was a pretty place, peaceful and welcoming. As Josie's gaze shifted back to the old stables, she was distracted by a movement in the bushes beside her. To Josie's surprise, a little girl climbed out from the middle of them. She had long curly brown hair, a snub nose, and dark blue eyes, which she fixed on Josie.

"Hello," Josie said, a little taken aback by this sudden appearance.

"I'm Ellie Carter," the little girl announced. "I live here. I was six last week!" she finished proudly.

"Congratulations! I'm Josie Grace," Josie began. "I live—"

"I know where you live," Ellie interrupted. "I've seen you before."

"Have you?" Josie asked, surprised.

Ellie folded her arms. "Yes." She turned her dark eyes warily on Josie. "You've got a gray horse," she said solemnly.

"That's right." Josie nodded her head. "Her name is Charity." Suddenly Josie remembered the rustling of leaves in the bushes when she had been in Charity's field the night before. "Wait a minute," she said slowly, smiling down at Ellie. "Have you been spying on me?"

"How did you know?" Ellie said, looking slightly deflated.

"Oh, I have my ways," Josie replied mysteriously.

"Did you see me watching you last night?" asked Ellie.

"So it *was* you!" Josie exclaimed. "I thought it was a rabbit."

Ellie grinned triumphantly. "No, that was me. I

found a great spy hole in the hedge at the bottom of the lawn."

"So you've seen Charity," Josie said, smiling as Barker came sniffing around her heels.

"Yes—" Ellie began. She bent down suddenly and scooped Barker up into her arms. "Hello, puppy. You want to play, don't you?" she cuddled the little dog and turned back to Josie. "Come on," she said, grabbing her hand and tugging insistently. "Let's go play in the back."

Josie had to jog to keep up with the little girl.

Mrs. Grace and Ellie's mom were still talking and Ellie kept up a steady stream of chatter as she led Josie across the rolling lawn. "This yard's a lot bigger than the one at my old house," she called over her shoulder to Josie. "It's even got a stream. Look."

They had reached the bank where overhanging trees bent down to meet the shallow stream. Josie saw a small checked blanket spread out on the grass. A pretty doll sat on it in front of a plate piled high with grass and leaves.

"This is Isabel," Ellie pointed to the doll. "Isabel, this is Josie. We're having a picnic," she told Josie.

Josie pointed at the plate. "That looks tasty," she said solemnly.

"Grass sandwiches," Ellie announced.

"Mmmm, my favorite," Josie smiled. "What a beautiful doll. Is she new?"

"Yes." Ellie threw herself down on the blanket and Josie stretched out on the grass beside her, tilting her face up to soak in the warm sun.

Ellie stroked the doll's blond, wavy hair. "My best friend Laura gave her to me as a good-bye present," she explained. "I don't live near Laura anymore." Suddenly Ellie looked sad and gave a little sigh. "I guess Isabel is my best friend now."

Josie felt sorry for the little girl. She sat up and began to tell Ellie about her move. "I've only been here a few months myself," she said. "It felt strange at first, and I was a bit sad."

Ellie was immediately interested. "Why were you sad?" she asked.

"Oh, because I was lonely and I had to find new homes for the three horses we used to have," Josie explained.

"You had three horses?" Ellie asked.

Josie nodded. "Yes, Faith, Hope, and Charity. We

found great homes for Faith and Hope. And it turned out I was able to keep Charity."

"I was allowed to bring Barker with me." Ellie sat up on her knees. They both turned to watch the little puppy as he turned circles on the grass, playing tag with his own tail. "He's so silly," Ellie said, giggling.

"He's adorable," Josie added. She turned eagerly to the little girl. "If you like animals, Ellie, you are always welcome to come and visit Charity. You don't have to spy on her from behind the bushes, you know."

Ellie fiddled with Isabel's hair. "Maybe," she said slowly, and Josie noticed the younger girl looked really nervous. Then she smiled brightly. "Do you want to have a tea party? Isabel wants some more sandwiches."

Josie agreed, happy to see Ellie cheering up. "Do you think I can have some juice to go with this food?" Josie asked, grabbing a plastic cup and walking over to the stream. She bent down and scooped up some of the water, then carried it back to Ellie. "For Madam Isabel," she announced gravely. "Fresh apple juice."

Ellie laughed. "That's her favorite!"

* * *

The crunch of tires on gravel made both girls look up from their game.

"Daddy!" cried Ellie. She ran over to meet her father, whose arms were filled with grocery bags. Josie made her way over to say hello.

"Sam," Mrs. Carter said to her husband. "This is Mary Grace and her daughter, Josie. They're our neighbors."

Sam Carter held out his hand. "Pleased to meet you," he said. It was obvious to Josie where Ellie got her curly brown hair and dark blue eyes from just by looking at the smiling man.

Ellie flung her arms around her dad's waist. "Josie's played tea party with me and she brought us some chocolate brownies," she declared. "And she's coming to see me again, aren't you, Josie?" She turned to look at Josie.

"Of course." Josie grinned. "I can never pass up a grass sandwich!"

As they walked back home, Mrs. Grace filled Josie in on what she had learned about the Carters.

"Sam Carter is a doctor. He starts work at the Littlehaven Hospital next week," she told Josie.

Wilton Public Library

Wilton Public Library
PO Box 447
Wilton, IA 52778

"Will Ellie go to school around here?" Josie asked. They had reached the edge of Charity's field and the gray horse was standing waiting for them. Josie felt in her pocket for a stray treat and gave it to Charity, who nuzzled the palm of her hand with her soft lips.

"Yes," Mrs. Grace said, reaching up to tickle Charity's ears. "She starts at the local school in September." She paused thoughtfully. "Actually, I get the impression that her mom is a bit worried about her."

"Why's that?" Josie asked. "No, Charity," she said, laughing as the horse sniffed around her pockets. "I haven't got any more. Sorry. I'll bring you some later, I promise." The horse gave the pockets one last sniff and returned her attention to the grass.

"Well, Ellie's just moved from a big city, where she had lots of friends, to the country, where she doesn't know anyone," Mrs. Grace continued. "Her mother thinks she'll be lonely."

"Well, she knows me now," Josie said, giving Charity an affectionate pat good-bye. "And I'll introduce her to Charity, too. What could be better than having a horse for a friend?"

Wilton Public Library
108 E. 4th St., Box 447
Wilton, IA 52778
(563) 732-2583

CHAPTER FOUR

The next morning, Josie checked to see if the mail had arrived. She was waiting for the new issue of her favorite horse magazine.

Basil was barking at the door. So Josie knew that he was anxious to tear through the stack of letters. Basil loved to get his teeth into the mail. Saving mail from Basil's greedy mouth was a daily job. Whoever opened the door had to guard the letters from him. But by now it had become a game and, Josie had to admit, she kind of enjoyed it. She scratched his scruffy brown-and-white coat. "Better luck next time, Basil," she said. "You'll have to run faster than that if you're going to beat me." Basil looked up at her and wagged his tail furiously. Just wait until tomorrow, he seemed to be saying. Josie couldn't help laughing at his determined expression.

She walked into the kitchen where her dad was making breakfast. "Did you rescue the mail?" he asked over his shoulder.

Josie smiled proudly. "Of course," she said. "After all, I am the champion mail grabber."

Mr. Grace wiped his hands on a towel. "So it's got nothing to do with the fact that your legs are about ten times longer than Basil's?"

"My legs may be longer, but Basil's got two more than me, so that just about makes us even," Josie replied triumphantly. She began to sort through the pile of mail she still held in her hand. "Two for mom. One for you." She handed a brown envelope to her dad. "All right! My horse magazine!" Josie tore off the plastic wrap and began to flick through the pages. She was about to start an exciting horse rescue story when her dad sighed loudly.

"What's wrong, Robert?" Mrs. Grace said, coming into the room. "More bills?"

Mr. Grace looked up from his letter. "No, it's from a geography survey company. It seems they need to run tests on the pipes in our backyard. They'll have to dig up the field to run the tests. They say here that it might take a month or two."

"In the middle of summer?" Mrs. Grace groaned. "There goes all our peace and quiet."

Josie had almost finished the story when something suddenly clicked in her head. "Hang on a minute, Dad," she said, looking up from the page. "Did you say they'll have to dig up the field?"

Mr. Grace looked at the letter again. "Yes, that's right."

"Charity's field?" Josie was dismayed. "But then where will Charity go?"

Mr. Grace scratched his head. "That's a bit of a problem," he admitted. "A few weeks is a long time to be homeless when you're a horse."

"I suppose we'll just have to move her, sweetie," Mrs. Grace said gently. "Perhaps Lonsdale Stables could take her? Charity has been there before."

"But Lonsdale is miles away," Josie wailed. "You'd have to drive me all the time. I probably wouldn't get to see Charity every day." Suddenly the summer didn't look so good. She had been looking forward to spending the whole summer with her horse. But without Charity right in her backyard, the summer just wouldn't be the same. The thought made Josie miserable.

"How long before they start?" Mrs. Grace asked. "Less than a week, did you say? We'll have to come up with a solution." She reached for her keys on the kitchen counter. "Look, we'll talk about it more later," she promised. "I have to run, or I'll be late. I'm going to ride Connie this morning." Connie was a beautiful black mare that Mrs. Grace sometimes exercised for her friend Jane.

Mr. Grace put a consoling arm around Josie. "Don't worry," he said. "We'll find a temporary home for Charity. But you'll probably have to face the fact that it won't be as close to home as where she is now."

Josie barely ate any breakfast. All she wanted to do was get outside to see Charity. As Josie walked out her back door, her heart sank. Seeing her horse grazing just a few feet away was such a beautiful sight. Not having Charity nearby would make the summer unbearable.

There was a slight rustling near the bushes and Josie turned slowly. She quietly made her way over to the hedge. "Boo!" Josie cried, and Ellie leaped up in surprise. "I gotcha," Josie said, laughing.

Suddenly Josie realized that Ellie looked a little guilty and a bit frightened.

"I was just teasing," Josie said gently. "You don't have to spy on us, you know. Why don't you come and meet Charity? She's very friendly."

But Ellie was already off and running. "You can't catch me," she cried over her shoulder.

"Oh, yes, I can," Josie called as she set off after Ellie, her own worries momentarily forgotten.

After an intense game of tag, Josie and Ellie sat down on the patio for some cold drinks. Ellie was showing Josie some new clothes she had just gotten for Isabel. "Look, Josie, she's even got her own swimsuit." Ellie held up a pink stripy suit. Although Josie was still worried about Charity, she couldn't help but smile at Ellie.

Suddenly, Mrs. Carter's voice interrupted her thoughts. "Are you two girls having fun?"

Josie shaded her eyes against the sun's glare as she looked up at Ellie's mom. "Yes, thanks. The lemonade is delicious."

While Ellie played with Isabel, Mrs. Carter slid into the empty seat next to Josie. "I want to thank you for being so good with Ellie," she said quietly. "It's really helping her to settle in, having you as a friend. I know she's half your age, but I hope you don't think hanging around with her as too much of a chore."

Josie smiled. "Not at all. It's fun. I know what it feels like to move, although I didn't have to change schools as well. My dad's a teacher, and he says the school that Ellie's going to is great and that the kids are very nice."

"Yes, I've heard that." Mrs. Carter sounded relieved. "I think Ellie will feel a lot more settled once she starts school. Although I don't want to wish summer over too soon!"

She smiled at Josie. "Do you have any exciting plans?"

"Only to ride Charity every day," Josie said with determination. *If she's here*, she added silently to herself.

Anna sat cross-legged on Josie's bed, munching on popcorn. Her dark eyes were screwed up in concentration and her straight black hair fell forward over her face. The girls had been talking about just one thing all night—Charity. The Graces still hadn't decided where Charity was going to go, and Anna and Josie were no nearer to solving the problem. Still, as Anna pointed out, as she was sleeping over, they had all night to talk about it.

"What we need," Anna declared now, "is a plan of action."

Josie reached over to grab some of the buttery popcorn. "Sounds good," she said. "Hey, Anna, leave some of this for me."

"Oh, sorry." Anna pushed the bowl toward her friend. "Hand me that pen and paper on your desk, Josie. I'll make a list. Let's start with all the places you could possibly keep Charity. You make the suggestions, and I'll give the pros and cons."

"Good idea," Josie agreed. "But you have to say no to my first suggestion." She paused and Anna waited expectantly. "Lonsdale," Josie finally said.

"Oh, that's a definite no," Anna agreed. "Too far away. Next."

Josie thought for a moment. "Um, my backyard?"

"Too overgrown. Lots of dangerous horse plants

in there," Anna warned seriously, shaking her head.

"Your backyard?" Josie was starting to get silly.

Anna giggled. "Nice try, but too small."

Josie racked her brains. "Jill Atterbury's field," she said triumphantly.

"Not bad," Anna said slowly. "How about it?"

"That's no good either," Josie whispered. "I'd still have to rely on a ride, and it would be too much for Jill to look after Charity as well as Faith if I couldn't get there every day."

"Too bad there aren't any spare fields around here you could use or rent," Anna said, giving up on the list.

Josie sighed. "I know."

"All you need is some land," Anna went on. "And a stall."

"A stall," Josie repeated, lost in thought. "Wait a minute!" She thought back to her morning spent with Ellie. Of course! There were *two* little stables, tucked away in the courtyard of Ellie's house. Josie turned to Anna and beamed. "You've just given me the perfect idea! You're a genius."

"That's what I keep saying," Anna said modestly. "So, spill the beans. What's this brilliant idea of mine? I mean yours." She flicked some popcorn at Josie.

Excitedly, Josie began to tell Anna about Ellie Carter. Anna didn't understand at first, but as soon as Josie got to the part about the courtyard, everything clicked. "There are two old stables just sitting there, Anna," Josie said, her eyes shining with excitement. "They look like they haven't been used in a while, but I'm sure with a few repairs and some paint, one of them would make a perfect temporary home for Charity. And it would be perfect for me, too. It would mean that Charity would be right next door! I could still ride her every day."

"It's perfect," agreed Anna. "Do you think the Carters will say yes?"

"I don't see why not," Josie said. "Ellie is always spying on Charity. And who wouldn't want Charity for a friend?"

"Then I think we have our plan of action!" Anna declared.

"Come on, let's go and tell my mom," Josie said as she ran across her room toward the stairs.

"Wait for me!" Anna cried. She jumped off the bed and ran downstairs behind Josie.

* * *

Mrs. Grace was reading a newspaper by the fireplace when Josie and Anna rushed into the living room. Breathlessly, Josie explained their idea.

"Well, I have to say, it does sound like a very sensible solution," she said. She folded her paper and placed it on her lap. "I'll call Mrs. Carter tomorrow and discuss it with her."

"Can't you do it tonight?" Josie pleaded.

Mrs. Grace laughed at her daughter's impatience. "No, honey, I'm sorry. It's too late now. I promise I'll do it first thing after breakfast," she said.

"How am I going to be able to wait that long?" groaned Josie. "I definitely won't be able to sleep now."

"Well, if we're not sleeping, we are definitely going to need more food," declared Anna.

"Anyone for Mexican chili chocolate cake?" Mr. Grace asked, his head popping around the door.

"Good timing, Dad," Josie said with a laugh as she and Anna followed him into the kitchen. "Another perfect plan."

CHAPTER
FIVE

Josie woke up the next morning to Anna shaking her arm. "Come on, sleepyhead," she said. "It's late. I need some breakfast. I'm starving."

The smell of pancakes drifted up from the kitchen as Josie and Anna walked downstairs. In the hallway, Mrs. Grace was talking on the telephone. Josie paused on the stairs and held her breath as she caught a bit of the conversation.

"Thank you, Jenny. I'll wait to hear from you," her mother was saying. "Good-bye." Mrs. Grace hung up the phone and turned to Josie. "That was Jenny Carter, Ellie's mother," she explained.

Josie couldn't stand the suspense any longer.

"Well, what did she say?" she demanded. "Can they take Charity?"

"When do we start painting?" Anna asked eagerly.

Mrs. Grace shook her head. "Hold on, girls. Not right away, I'm afraid," she said. "Mrs. Carter is a little unsure of the idea and wants some time to think about it."

Josie's stomach lurched. "Why?" she asked in dismay. "It's the perfect solution. Plus, there's nowhere else for Charity to go."

Mr. Grace emerged from the kitchen carrying a plate full of pancakes. "Why don't you tell us the news while we eat these nice, warm pancakes," Mr. Grace suggested.

The pancakes smelled delicious and Anna dug in, but Josie didn't feel like eating. She pushed her food around the plate as she listened to her mother relate the conversation with Mrs. Carter.

"It seems that Ellie is actually quite scared of horses," Mrs. Grace explained. "Just about a year ago, a horse she was riding spooked at something and bolted. Ellie fell off and broke her arm. She was in a cast for weeks, and since then she's been afraid of horses."

"But it wasn't entirely the horse's fault that Ellie fell off," Josie butted in.

Mrs. Grace smiled at her. "No, Josie, I'm sure it wasn't. But Ellie would have been too young to understand that. All she knows is that the horse caused her pain. And when you're very small, even a little horse can seem big and scary." She paused to take a sip of coffee before continuing. "Remember, Josie, you've been lucky enough to grow up around horses, and they've all been gentle."

Josie thought for a moment. "So that's why Ellie doesn't want to get too close to Charity!" she exclaimed. "Now all that hiding behind the bushes and spying makes more sense."

"But if she's spying on Charity, she's obviously curious," Anna pointed out, as she buttered a piece of toast. "And if she's ridden horses before, she must like them."

"That's true," Josie said thoughtfully. "Maybe Ellie just needs a chance to spend some time with Charity. Then she'll see how great and gentle she is." She raised her fork triumphantly. "It's the perfect plan to cure Ellie's fear. After that, she'll definitely want Charity to stay. The problem is solved!"

"Hang on a minute." Mrs. Grace turned her eyes to Josie. "It's the Carters' decision," she said. "Sometimes people are genuinely scared of horses, and it doesn't help to push them. Mrs. Carter promised to talk to her husband and Ellie. We have to leave it up to them." Then, seeing Josie's downcast expression, her tone softened. "I'm sorry, sweetie," she continued, "you'll just have to wait and see what they say."

Anna gave her friend's arm a sympathetic squeeze. "Just try to stay positive. Mrs. Carter didn't say no, did she? That's got to be a good sign." Anna paused, a piece of toast halfway to her mouth. "Of course, it could be that she was stalling for time—too embarrassed to refuse right away." Anna had a habit of saying exactly what she thought without thinking.

Josie shot her a dismayed glance.

"Sorry," Anna said quickly. "I'll just eat my breakfast and not talk."

After breakfast, Anna went home and Josie tried to find something to do. She flicked through magazines. She started to read her new book. She even thought about finishing off her summer project for school. But every time the phone rang she jumped as if she had been stung by a bee. She kept hoping it would be Mrs. Carter to say that Charity could stay with them. It never was. Once it was Jill's mother to say that she'd heard there was a space available at Lonsdale and to call if they wanted it for Charity. Another time it was Mrs. Grace's friend, Jane, asking when Mary would like to ride Connie again. Then Anna called to find out it if there was any news.

"Not a word," Josie wailed. "This is awful, Anna."

"Well, this should cheer you up," Anna said. "Mom wants you to come help out with the pony rides at the Friendship House Festival. Hope's going to be giving rides to all the children and Zoe's away visiting her mom, so they need an extra pair of hands. I'll be there too. Ben's got a tennis game or he'd be there, too."

"That's a great idea," Josie agreed. "Of course I'll help."

As soon as she put the phone down, Josie decided to take Charity out for a ride to get her mind off things. "Maybe when I come back Mom will have heard something," she said to herself as she walked down to Charity's field, knowing the sight of her horse would cheer her up.

Charity whinnied softly when she saw Josie approaching, and rested her gray nose on the gate. She looked at Josie with big, gentle, brown eyes. "You're such a sweetheart," Josie whispered into her ear. "How could anyone be afraid of you?" She sighed loudly and leaned her head against the horse. "Oh, the Carters have to take you, Charity. They just have to."

The long ride did its job and Josie was feeling much better by the time she got back home. The weather had been perfect, the fields were in great shape, and Charity had been eager to be off. They'd cantered for a while, and Josie's mind had drifted along, happy just to be riding. For an hour she had almost forgotten that by next week Charity might be homeless. Her peace was shattered the minute she saw Ellie and her mother coming toward her.

Josie's heart began to race. Perfect timing, she thought. She patted Charity on the neck. "I'm going to introduce you to the Carters, Charity, and you have to be on your best behavior." Charity's ears twitched back and forth as if she was actually listening to every word.

Josie jumped lightly out of the saddle. "I think I'd better lead you over, Charity. It looks less threatening," she explained to the horse. "We don't want to take any chances with Ellie. She's scared of horses, you know."

Up ahead, Josie could see Mrs. Carter and Ellie. Ellie was clutching her mother's hand tightly and Mrs. Carter seemed to be reassuring her that everything was fine. For a moment Josie worried they might turn around without giving Charity a chance, but she was relieved to see that Mrs. Carter was actually smiling at her. Ellie peered shyly out from behind her mother.

"Hi, Josie," Mrs. Carter said cheerfully. "It's nice to see you. This must be Charity. She's beautiful." Charity blew softly through her nose, as if in agreement.

Josie brought Charity to a halt. "Thank you. We just got back from a ride," she explained.

"Can I pet her?" asked Mrs. Carter.

"Of course," Josie replied. "She's very friendly. She really loves to be scratched on the nose."

Mrs. Carter moved closer and began to make a fuss over Charity. Charity stood still, basking in the attention. Meanwhile, Ellie hung back, watching with wide eyes, but making no move to come forward.

Josie turned to her. "Would you like to pet her?" she asked Ellie. Ellie shook her head shyly. Mrs. Carter stepped back and put an arm around her daughter. "It's all right, Ellie," she reassured her. "Charity's very friendly. And she's so pretty. Feel how soft her nose is."

Ellie shifted from one foot to the other. "I'll pet her," she said in a small voice. "If you're sure it's safe."

"Charity wouldn't hurt a fly," Josie said seriously.

"She is big, though, isn't she?" Ellie said, looking up at the horse.

Josie smiled. "She is bigger than you, but so am I, and I'm your friend, aren't I?"

Ellie nodded slowly. "Yes," she said quietly.

"Charity is very gentle," Josie continued. "There's nothing to be afraid of." She looked at the little girl's doubtful face. "And I'll hold the reins the whole time. I promise."

"Okay," Ellie said. Slowly she walked forward, one hand holding tightly to her mother's, the other cautiously reaching out to touch Charity's nose. Josie held her breath and watched. Please let it be all right, she thought. A smile spread across Ellie's face as she felt the soft hairs on Charity's muzzle. "She's tickling my hand," she gasped and laughed.

Josie breathed out slowly and began to relax. It was clear that Ellie was enjoying herself and making friends with Charity. Charity wanted to be friendly too, because she dropped her head to nuzzle Ellie's shoulder. But the sight of Charity's gray nose lunging downward startled Ellie. She jumped back in fright, and Charity, surprised by the sudden movement, tossed her head in the air. Josie's hand was momentarily pulled skyward. She quickly tugged Charity's head down, but it was too late. The damage was done. Ellie was once again hiding behind her mother's legs.

"I didn't like that," she said anxiously.

"I'm so sorry," Josie said. "Charity didn't mean anything. She was just trying to make friends."

"She looked scary," wailed Ellie.

"She's calmer now," said Mrs. Carter. "Look, Ellie, she's perfectly safe to pet."

Josie smiled gratefully at Mrs. Carter as she patted Charity's neck. But Ellie looked far from convinced.

Mrs. Carter turned to Josie. "I'm sorry, Josie," she said with an apologetic shrug. "I don't think Ellie's ready for this yet. I'd better take her home."

Josie watched them leave. As they walked away, Ellie held on tightly to her mother's hand and did not look back.

Josie began to lead Charity back to the barn so she could finish cooling her off. "I think we blew it, Charity," she muttered, as she groomed the horse's gray coat. Charity hung her head and blew softly through her nose. Josie couldn't help laughing at her mournful expression. "It wasn't your fault," she said. The only question is, if they don't take you, who will? Josie thought, as she brushed out Charity's white tail with gentle strokes. It looked like it was time for a new plan of action.

CHAPTER
SIX

Josie tugged on her stubborn riding boot. She was trying to get ready to go to the Friendship House festival. While pulling at her boot, she was telling her mother all about meeting the Carters out in front of their house with Charity. "Mrs. Carter said Ellie wasn't ready to make friends with Charity yet," she said with a big sigh.

Mrs. Grace put her arm around Josie. "I'm sorry, sweetie," she said. "I suppose to a small girl like Ellie, Charity is just another big, scary horse, even if *we* know how gentle she is. I think you are probably right about the Carters not wanting to stable her," she continued. "Mrs. Carter was pretty wary on the phone. This incident may have just been the icing on the cake. It's such a shame that Ellie is so scared."

Josie nodded her head. "I can't think of anything worse than being frightened of horses."

Her mother smiled at her. "Never mind. We've still got Lonsdale Riding Stable as an option. We know Charity will be well looked after there, and I promise," she added, seeing Josie's glum expression, "we'll take you to see her as often we can. It's not for that long, anyway." The telephone interrupted their conversation and Mrs. Grace headed off to answer it.

"It's a pity Lonsdale isn't next door," Josie muttered under her breath.

The sound of a horn outside made Josie run for the door. Anna waved from the backseat of her mom's car. "Hurry up, slowpoke!" she called. "We've got some pony rides to organize."

"Coming! Bye, Mom!" she called over her shoulder as she left the house.

Josie climbed into the back seat next to Anna. "Any news on Charity?" she asked eagerly, as soon as Josie was settled.

Josie shook her head sadly. Quickly she filled Anna in on what had happened with Ellie.

Anna groaned sympathetically. "Oh, that was such bad luck," she moaned.

"Mom thinks the best option is Lonsdale," Josie said with a sigh.

"It's so far away," Anna said.

"And expensive, too," Josie added. "I know my folks are worried about the money."

They sat in silence for the rest of the trip. When they finally arrived at Friendship House, though, their bad moods vanished. Brightly colored flags lined the driveway, paper windmills dotted the lawn, and, on the terrace of Friendship House itself, a trio of musicians played catchy tunes.

"This looks amazing," Josie declared happily.

"Wait until you see the art show. It's awesome," Anna promised.

Lynne parked the car around the side of the house. A slim, brown-haired young woman made her way through the crowd to meet them.

"Hi, Liz." Lynne smiled. "I've brought some reinforcements." She nodded at Anna and Josie.

"Excellent!" Liz Tallant, who ran Friendship House, beamed at the girls. "I think there will be a lot of children wanting a pony ride today." She turned to gesture at all the people. Children were chasing balloons and somersaulting on the grass. Grown-ups sat chatting and munching on carnival food.

"Hi, Lynne." An excited voice made its way over the other voices. A small, blond-haired boy came rushing over.

"Hi, there, Max," Lynne said, smiling down at the bouncing bundle of energy.

Max looked up at her eagerly. "Can I show Mom and Dad my pictures?" he pleaded.

A young couple walked up behind him. "It's all my son has been talking about," the man said, laughing.

Lynne smiled and glanced at her watch. "We'll have the grand opening of the art show in five minutes," she announced. "But I think I can arrange a sneak preview. Max's paintings are just great. Why don't you follow me?"

As Max and his parents followed Lynne over to the art studio, Liz turned to Josie and Anna.

"Would you girls mind tacking up Hope?" she asked. "We need to get going on those rides."

Josie and Anna walked over to Hope's stall. On

the way, they passed Jack and Jill, the resident donkeys. Children were hanging onto the fence, enthusiastically patting the cuddly gray pair.

"Why don't we do donkey rides, too?" Anna wondered.

"They're too unpredictable," Josie said. "These kids need something steady and reliable." Hope whinnied loudly as Josie approached. She reached up to put her arms around the horse's gray neck and kiss her funny bent nose. "And I think Hope is the perfect horse for the job."

A few hours and a lot of children later, Josie slipped the saddle off Hope's back.

"She's certainly earned her rest," Anna observed. "Those rides were popular."

"She is wonderful," Josie agreed, brushing her fingers through Hope's mane fondly.

Anna grabbed the brush box and, together, the two girls brushed Hope and made sure she was comfortable after her day of hard work. Then they turned her out, and she immediately went to stand lazily in the shade of a large old oak tree.

The friends stood watching Hope for a moment and Josie fell silent.

Anna looked at her curiously. "What's the matter?" she asked gently.

Josie sighed. "I was just thinking about how special Hope is. There were so many children today, and a lot of them were very rowdy and noisy, but Hope didn't seem to mind one bit."

"Hope is perfect for Friendship House," Anna agreed. "Charity wouldn't have done well here. She's Hope's daughter, but she's got a mischievous streak. Still, that's what you love about her. If Ellie can't see how great she is, then that's her problem."

Josie smiled at Anna. Anna was a good friend and could always be counted on to say the loyal thing. "It's true," she said. "There isn't a mean bone in Charity's body, but Ellie's got to figure that out herself. I'll just have to find somewhere else for Charity to stay on my own."

"Well, you found perfect homes for Hope and Faith! This should be a piece of cake. Let's go check out the art show."

The art studio was in an airy, modern extension of the main house. Inside, Lynne Marshall was sorting through some paintings on the table in front of her, while several parents wandered around the room looking at the pictures that covered the walls. One little girl was proudly showing her parents her colorful picture of a pond.

"I think this one's my favorite," Anna said, leading Josie to a large painting. An abstract design of circles and swirly shapes leaped energetically across the canvas. "Look at those fantastic pinks and reds, and that big bright yellow circle in the center. It reminds me of summer."

"It's great," Josie agreed. "The colors are just gorgeous."

"The show is officially a hit," Lynne told the girls, smiling contentedly. Josie wandered around the room, examining the work on the walls. A small painting of a familiar-looking horse caught her eye. It was Hope. She leaned in closer to examine the picture.

"I love this one," she said delightedly. Lynne came over to stand behind her.

"Isn't it good?" she agreed. "It was done by Max, the little boy you met earlier."

"He's painted Hope perfectly," Josie said. She

gazed at the painting for a while longer. Suddenly Josie had the feeling that everything would be all right. Anna was right. Somewhere out there was the perfect place for Charity. Josie just had to find it.

Josie waved good-bye to Anna and Lynne and walked around the side of her house into the backyard. It was a beautiful summer afternoon and even though she had had fun at Friendship House, she was starting to feel gloomy again. The idea of not being able to see Charity every day was eating away at her. For the first time in a while she desperately missed her old home. "This never would have happened if we hadn't moved."

The bang of a van door interrupted her thoughts. She looked up to see one of the workmen waving at her from the end of the driveway.

"We've finished for today," he called. "Can you tell your mom we'll be back first thing Tuesday?"

That leaves only four days to find Charity a home, Josie thought, as she forced a smile on her face and nodded her head.

She looked over at Charity and noticed that she was trotting up and down along the fence. "Poor

Charity," Josie said, walking over to her. "Did those workmen bother you? You can probably tell something is up, can't you?"

Charity continued walking back and forth beside the fence, dropping her head as she tracked along the grass. Josie followed her gaze right to Ellie's spy hole. But it wasn't Ellie hiding in the bushes. Instead, as she drew closer, Josie saw Isabel's face peering through the hole. Josie shooed Charity gently away and peeked over the fence to see Ellie crouching down, holding Isabel up to the spy hole.

"Hi there," Josie said softly.

Ellie looked up and hugged her doll to her. "Isabel wanted to see Charity," she whispered.

"Oh, really," Josie smiled. "Well, Charity doesn't mind."

Ellie scrambled to her feet and looked at Josie. "Isabel isn't as scared of horses as I am," she said in a small voice.

"Isabel's very brave," Josie said firmly. "And so are you for bringing her over here."

"Charity was just saying hello to Isabel, wasn't she?" said Ellie. "She wasn't going to eat her, was she?"

Josie laughed. "I don't think so," she said

reassuringly. "Charity doesn't like the taste of dolls. She prefers grass. Look." She pointed to Charity who stood munching contentedly on some grass in the far corner of the field.

"She's eating grass sandwiches, just like Isabel!" Ellie exclaimed, her eyes lighting up. "I gotta go, see ya', Josie," she called and ran off, swinging her doll high into the air as she went.

Josie watched her go and, for a moment, felt better. Ellie seemed okay. She hadn't mentioned the earlier incident and she was still spying on Charity. But Ellie still didn't seem comfortable with Charity face-to-face.

Josie knew her mom had been right when she said that no one could force Ellie to be friends with Charity, but she couldn't help feeling frustrated that there was nothing more she could do. And not just so that Charity could stay next door, but for Ellie's sake as well. Josie knew that Charity could be a friend for the lonely little girl. She knew it.

Josie was just walking in the door when her mother appeared at the door. "How was your day?" she asked Josie.

"Great," Josie said. "It was good to see Hope. Friendship House is, well, it's so friendly!" she finished. Her mother laughed, and Josie looked at her curiously. "You look happy," she said.

"Relieved, more like it." Mrs. Grace sighed. "And you will be, too, when I tell you the news."

"What news?" Josie asked quickly. She followed her mother into the kitchen.

Mrs. Grace folded her arms. "Well," she began. "We found a place for Charity."

"Where?" Josie asked curiously.

Mrs. Grace reached down into the cupboard for two glasses, which she placed on the counter in front of her. "Mrs. Carter called earlier," she said, pouring a glass of juice. "She's agreed that you can keep Charity at their house, after all."

Josie was amazed. "Really? After what happened before? I thought we'd blown it for sure."

"Apparently not," Mrs. Grace said, watching Josie take a big gulp of juice. "You, *or* Charity, must have done something right. Mrs. Carter said she thought Charity was a sweetheart." Mrs. Grace stopped. She looked over at Josie, who was just staring out the window at the Carters' house. "Josie?"

"What? Oh, sorry." Josie said, and grinned. "I'm just in shock that Charity has the perfect place to stay. What made the Carters change their minds?"

"I think Mrs. Carter realizes that Ellie's fear of horses is a real problem," her mother explained. "It wasn't so obvious when they lived in the city, but now that they are in the country, Ellie is going to have to get used to them—and the Carters seem to think that Charity is the perfect way to start."

Josie nodded. "She's definitely going to come across horses sooner or later," she agreed.

"Exactly," Mrs. Grace continued. "And Mrs. Carter has explained that to Ellie. Did you know Mrs. Carter used to ride? She hopes that Ellie will learn to enjoy it as much as she did. *And* if she went to a local stable, it would be a great way for her to make some new friends."

"Charity might help her overcome her fears!" Josie declared.

Her mother nodded her head. "She might," she agreed. "Let's just hope it works."

"Of course it will," Josie cried. "Charity could give anyone confidence."

"There is a 'but' to all this, you know, Josie," her mother warned.

"Oh, what's that?" Josie looked worried.

Mrs. Grace smiled. "I said we would repaint the stables so that the Carters could keep more horses there permanently, if they want to at a later date—if things work out. Oh, and when I say *we*, I really mean *you*, Josie. I'll help out, but Charity is your horse and this is your project."

"I'll do it." Josie grinned. "Although I probably will need a little help. May I use the phone, Mom?"

Mrs. Grace nodded and laughed as Josie raced to call Anna. Anna immediately agreed to come over that weekend and help Josie fix up the stables. "Ben will come, too, Josie, I know he'll want to help," Anna added. "And I'll see if my mom can help. After all, she is a qualified painter and decorator."

"That would be great, Anna," Josie said excitedly. "We've only got four days to get things ready, though," she warned. "The workmen came today, and they'll be back on Tuesday."

"Phew, that's not long!" Anna exclaimed. "But I will do it, no problem!"

"See you then," Josie finished. "I'm going to tell Charity the good news."

Josie rushed out the back door and down to the field. Charity seemed to sense her excitement, for she immediately trotted up to the gate to meet Josie. Josie flung her arms around the horse's silver-gray neck and hugged her as she explained what was going to happen. "You'll be happy at the Carters'," Charity," she promised. "We'll make it a real home away from home."

CHAPTER
SEVEN

It was early on Saturday morning, and Josie and her friends had wasted no time getting to work on Charity's new home. The workmen were due to start digging up her field on Tuesday morning, so the paint had to be dry by then. It would mean a weekend of hard work, but Josie was looking forward to it. Now, instead of worrying about where Charity was to go, she was making a new home, and it was so close to her! Anna and Ben were excited, too. Lynne Marshall had brought them to Josie's house early that morning and, true to her word, Anna had packed her own paintbrush. "I'm not leaving until this stable is in top shape," she had promised Josie. "Even if it means working all night!"

Mrs. Carter had been impressed by their enthusiasm. "You're welcome to stay until everything is finished," she had offered. "It will be nice to have some life around the place."

Lynne Marshall had been as good as her word and had given the stables a thorough examination. Her positive response made Josie confident that the stables would be up and running in no time.

Josie smiled as she looked around at her friends. We are so lucky, Charity, she thought, to have friends like these.

The barking of a puppy interrupted her thoughts and she looked down to see Barker jumping around her heels. Ellie was not far behind. She was dressed in an old oversized shirt, her curly brown hair tied back and in her hand she carried a paintbrush. "Can I help?" she shyly asked Josie.

Josie was surprised and pleased to see Ellie. Mrs. Carter came up behind her daughter and put her hand on her shoulder. "I've been showing Ellie photos of the horses I used to ride when I was her age," she explained gently. "She was very interested to see them."

"One of them looked just like Charity," Ellie announced.

Josie beamed at her. "Of course you can help—the more the merrier."

Ellie pointed up to a little window in the eaves of the house. "That's my room," she said. "I can see the stables from there."

Maybe she's beginning to change her mind about Charity, Josie thought, and her heart soared. I'm sure Mrs. Carter was right. Having Charity living right under her nose might be just what Ellie needs.

"Hey, earth to Josie! Do you expect us to do all the work?" Anna called out.

"Sorry," Josie said and smiled apologetically.

"I've finished sanding this side already," Ben said. "Do you want me to do yours for you?"

Josie bent to pick up some of the rough paper and set to work, smoothing the sharp wooden door of the old stable. "Ben, you may be quick, but I bet I'm neater than you," she teased.

"My sanding is perfect," Ben said proudly, standing back to admire his handiwork. "Now, just wait until you see my painting."

"Will you two stop chatting and give me a

hand?" yelled Anna. "I stepped in the paint can and I can't get my foot out."

Lynne Marshall shook her head. "I think we'll need a week, not a weekend, to finish this job," she groaned.

But by the afternoon, the team had made great progress. Almost all the rough edges had been smoothed down. Lynne had done a good job of tightening the loose bolts, and Ellie had done her fair share of painting. It was a real treat to see Mrs. Carter coming toward them carrying a tray filled with sandwiches, fruit, and a big pitcher of cold lemonade.

"Come have some lunch," she called. "You all look like you could do with a break." She arranged everything on a big table in the courtyard. For a while, there was silence as everyone concentrated on the food. It was only when the last sandwich had been eaten and the lemonade pitcher was almost empty that they found the energy to talk. Ellie was the first to break the silence.

"I think Charity's going to like her new home," she said proudly.

Josie smiled at her. "Charity will love this place, Ellie. And we couldn't have done it without you."

"You've been very helpful," Lynne agreed. "In fact, we've all done a great job so far. We might even get this place ready by the end of the weekend."

The afternoon passed in a whirl of activity. But by the end of the day they were all getting tired.

"Come on," Lynne said, seeing their weary faces. "Five more minutes and we'll call it a day."

"I don't think I can paint another stroke," wailed Anna, dropping her brush to the ground.

Ben walked over to where she stood and looked at her work. "But you've almost finished that side," he pointed out encouragingly.

"I'm almost finished here, too," Josie called from the front of the barn where she was putting the finishing touches on the door.

"Let's make it a race," Ben suggested, looking from Anna to Josie. "The first to finish painting wins—"

"A big chocolate bar and the video of their choice," Josie shouted.

"A hot bath and a comfy bed," moaned Anna.

Ben laughed. "Ready, set, go!" he cried.

Josie set about applying the wood paint to the

door. With a groan, Anna picked up her brush and began dabbing at the side of the stable. Five minutes later, Josie put down her brush. "Finished!" she announced.

"Oh, I'm finished too," said Anna quickly.

"I'll be the judge of that," Ben declared, walking between the two. "What do you think, Ellie?" Ellie was washing out her brush under the garden hose, but turned to listen to Ben. "Come on over here to help me judge."

Ellie carefully inspected all the painting and then firmly announced her decision. "I think Josie won!"

"I do too," Ben agreed. "It was very close, but I must declare Josie Grace the winner of the painting competition!"

Anna flopped to the floor. "I give up," she groaned.

"Don't worry, Anna," Josie said, laughing. "I might save you a piece of chocolate, if you're nice."

By the time they stopped for the night, the stables were ready for the final coat of paint the next day. Ellie would have stayed longer, but her mother insisted it was time for her bath, and the others took that as their cue to leave. Lynne took Ben home and Anna went back to Josie's house to stay the night. Mrs. Grace had promised Josie she would look after Charity while they worked, but Josie and Anna still stopped off to say good night.

"I'm sorry I haven't been around much today, Charity," Josie said, stroking the horse's neck. "We've been building you a new home. You'll like it, though, I promise." Charity blew softly through her nose in reply.

The delicious smell of cooking came from the kitchen as they stepped in through the front door of the house. Mr. Grace came out to meet them, drying his hands on a towel. "Ah, the workers return," he remarked, smiling. "I've made dinner," he went on. "One of my specialties—baked lasagna."

"Yum, my favorite," said Anna. "I'm glad that I decided to stay."

The next morning it was Josie who woke Anna up. "Time to paint, sleepyhead!" Josie said to her sleeping friend.

"I can't move!" Anna said from under the covers. "I need more sleep."

"Come on," Josie pleaded. "It's for Charity!"

Anna sat up and smiled. "Okay, I'm up." She climbed out of bed slowly. "Do you think your dad can make us pancakes?"

"You bet!" Josie said.

Everyone returned to the stables and worked throughout the day. "I'm exhausted," Josie said wearily as the sun was beginning to set. She wiped a smear of paint from her cheek and pushed an auburn curl out of one eye. Every bone in her body ached from the hard work.

"Are we really finished?" asked Ellie.

Josie smiled down at her. "I think so, Ellie. Charity's stable is as good as done."

"It's better than that!" Anna exclaimed, standing back to admire the restored building. "It's perfect."

"All it needs is a horse looking out over the door," Ben agreed.

Lynne ran her hand over the woodwork to feel the paint. "It's still slightly tacky in places," she observed, "but it should be nice and dry by tomorrow morning. When do you have to bring Charity over?"

"Not until tomorrow evening," Josie replied.

"The workmen want to get started first thing on Tuesday morning."

"It should be completely dry and ready by then," Lynne assured her. "Charity will be all set."

"I'm sure she will," Josie agreed. "Thanks again for all the help, everyone."

"No problem," Lynne said, smiling. "We had a great time. Come on, you two," she turned to Ben and Anna. "Time to go home."

"I'll be back soon to visit Charity in her new home," Anna said to Josie as she waved good-bye.

"Bye!" Josie and Ellie shouted together as the Marshalls' car pulled out of the driveway.

Josie turned to Mrs. Carter, who stood behind Ellie. "I'll bring Charity over tomorrow night."

"Perfect," replied Mrs. Carter. "After all this work, we need to see whether the star of the show approves of her new home."

"I think she'll love it," said Ellie, nodding her head. "It's the perfect horse home."

Josie shot a look over at Mrs. Carter who raised a pair of crossed fingers. *Let's hope this works*, she seemed to be saying. Josie couldn't have agreed more.

* * *

The next day, Josie pushed a wheelbarrow full of clean straw over to the Carters', to fill Charity's stall. She mentally checked off what she already had there. There was a water bucket in one of the stalls, as well as a feed bucket. A haynet was slung over her shoulder, and she'd taken a pitchfork over earlier for mucking out. Josie also wanted to make sure the paint was completely dry before Charity moved in.

As she arrived in the courtyard, she saw Ellie, hanging around the front of the stables. When she spotted Josie with the wheelbarrow an anxious look flashed across her face. "Is that for Charity?" she asked quietly.

"Yes," Josie explained. "I'm going to put it on the floor of her stall."

Ellie looked at the straw for a moment. "So Charity's definitely coming over tonight?" she asked in a small voice.

"Yup." Josie glanced at Ellie's anxious face. "Come on," she said, taking the little girl's hand. "Want to see how to bed a stall?" She led Ellie to the door of the stall and they peeped inside. "You see that bucket full of fresh water? That's for Charity to drink. And that bucket, there"—Josie pointed to the corner—"is scrubbed really clean, so that Charity can eat her dinner from it."

"That's good," Ellie said solemnly. "I wouldn't want to eat my dinner off a dirty plate, and neither would Isabel."

Josie nodded. "I think everything is almost ready, except for one thing."

"What's that?" Ellie asked.

"Well, Charity needs a bed," explained Josie. "She can't sleep on that hard floor, can she?"

"Oh, no," said Ellie, seriously. "She'd be very uncomfortable."

"Exactly," Josie agreed. "That's why I've brought the straw. Would you like to help me make a bed for Charity?"

"Yes, please," said Ellie. "I'll make her the most comfortable bed ever."

Josie showed Ellie how to fork the straw onto the floor, and how to put the hay where Charity could reach it.

When they had finished, Ellie stepped back to admire her handiwork. "Everything's all set," she declared proudly.

"Would you like to help me bring her over here later on?" Josie asked, but Ellie shook her head.

"I think I'll just stay here and wait for you," she said quickly.

Josie nodded. It was enough that Ellie had helped with the stall. She knew better than to push things too far. Ellie would have plenty of time over the next few weeks to get to know Charity better.

Later that evening, Josie walked Charity over to the Carter house. Sure enough, Ellie was there waiting for them, standing nervously on the back steps of her house. Excited by her new surroundings, Charity pulled on the lead, anxious to investigate. Barker came running up to greet the newcomer, yapping loudly. The clatter of Charity's hooves echoed sharply on the driveway as she tried to sidestep the little puppy. To Josie's dismay, the noise seemed to alarm Ellie and she inched further up the steps.

"Don't worry," Josie called out quickly. "I've got the lead tight."

But Ellie shook her head. "Her hooves sound big and scary," she said. "Maybe I'll come see her later." And with that, she disappeared inside the house.

Josie tried not to worry too much about Ellie's reaction. She knew it would take some time before the little girl felt comfortable with the horse.

Instead, she concentrated on introducing Charity as gently as possible to her new surroundings. It didn't take long. After a few cautious sniffs, Charity turned around twice inside the stall, rolled, and then started munching on her hay.

Josie laughed. "Well you certainly have made yourself at home," she said, tickling the horse's nose. As she drew the bolt on the lower half of the door, leaving the top half open, she caught a glimpse of Ellie, watching curiously from her bedroom window.

"She's got a perfect view of you from up there, Charity," Josie whispered in the horse's ear as she left. "So be on your best behavior. I'll see you tomorrow morning. Good night. And good night to you too, Ellie," she added under her breath. "You and Charity will be friends soon enough."

The next morning, Josie walked over to the Carter house. Charity poked her head over the stall door as she heard Josie approaching. Josie smiled at her horse.

"Well, you certainly look happy," she said as she

unbolted the stable door. "And I expect you're hungry, too. Breakfast time!" She ducked under Charity's neck and around to the back of the stable where the food was temporarily stored. She shoveled some into the feed bucket and brought it around to the stall. As she looked up, she caught sight of Ellie in the courtyard, peering cautiously into the stable.

When she saw Josie, the little girl jumped back. "Oh, you scared me!" she exclaimed. "I couldn't see Charity and I wondered what had happened to her."

"I'm giving her breakfast," Josie explained with a smile. "How was her first night?"

"Great," Ellie said. "Charity was so quiet I almost forgot she was here. I got a nice surprise when I opened my bedroom window this morning and saw her looking over the stall door."

"I love seeing Charity first thing in the morning," Josie said. "Would you like to help me give her breakfast? I'll show you what to do," she added, when she saw the doubtful expression on the girl's face.

"I'll watch from here." She moved closer to the stall door. "What's in there?" she asked, pointing to the bucket Josie was holding.

"It's oats," Josie explained. "Kind of like cereal for horses."

Ellie wrinkled up her nose. "It looks like the oatmeal my mom makes me eat."

Josie laughed. "It's just like that," she agreed. "Full of nuts and grain and all sorts of healthy things."

"Yuck," Ellie shook her head. "Poor Charity."

"She likes it!" Josie exclaimed. She tipped the grain into the feed bucket. "Hang on a minute, you," she laughed, as Charity bent her head eagerly into the food. "Wait for your apples."

"Yum, I love apples," said Ellie.

"So does Charity," Josie told her. "She needs fruit, just like you do, Ellie. How many should we give her?"

"Two," Ellie said firmly.

"Good idea." Josie nodded and put two apples into the mix. "All set, Charity," she said. She patted the horse on the neck and slipped out of the stall. Closing the door behind her she turned to face Ellie. "Want to help next time?"

"Yes, please." The little girl looked up at her. "On one condition."

"What's that?" asked Josie, curiously.

Ellie grinned. "We give her three apples!"

"It's a deal." Josie laughed.

"So it's working out with Charity and Ellie?" Anna asked Josie as they caught the bus back from the movies on Sunday afternoon.

"It seems to be," said Josie happily. "I can't believe Charity has only been there for a few days. She seems so settled. And Ellie is getting braver all the time. She still won't get too close to Charity, but she loves helping me feed her. That's real progress."

"Good for her," Anna said, impressed.

"Charity really likes the Carters' stables," Josie said, and smiled. "She's getting spoiled rotten. Oh, here's my stop." She got up to go. "See you later, Anna."

"I'll give you a call," Anna replied with a wave.

Josie waved back and jumped off the bus. She walked the short way to her house, feeling happy. Everything was working out perfectly. As she walked around to her back door, much to her surprise, there was an unexpected visitor—a very tall, four-legged visitor!

CHAPTER
EIGHT

Josie stared in amazement. "How did you manage to get out?" she asked. She laughed and flung her arms around Charity. Charity nudged at Josie's pockets with her soft velvety nose.

"Oh, you think you deserve a treat now?" Josie said. "I don't think I should give you any until you explain yourself. What are you doing out of your stall?" Josie tried to look stern.

Josie was interrupted by the sound of footsteps on the driveway.

"Josie?" Mrs. Carter's anxious voice called out.

"Hi, Mrs. Carter!"

"Charity!" Mrs. Carter sighed. She looked

relieved to see the gray horse. "Charity's door was wide open and she'd completely vanished. We were all worried. Ellie is very upset."

"It's all right, Mrs. Carter," Josie quickly reassured her. "Charity's fine."

"Thank goodness for that." Mrs. Carter breathed a sigh of relief. "How did she get out?"

Josie thought for a moment. "Did you say the stall door was wide open?" she asked.

"Yes. It wasn't forced or kicked or anything," Mrs. Carter replied. "It looked like the bolt had been drawn back."

Josie groaned. "It doesn't surprise me. This has happened before," she admitted. "Charity learned to undo knots when we lived at School Farm. But she hasn't tried it recently, and I've never known her to undo a bolt before." Josie couldn't help laughing. "Obviously, I didn't count on having an escape artist. I'll bring her back and we can work on that door," she finished. "I'm sorry for the trouble, Mrs. Carter."

"That's all right." Mrs. Carter said, looking relieved. "As long as Charity is safe. Ellie will be thrilled to see her back. She's getting used to looking out her window and seeing Charity."

Mrs. Carter headed back up the driveway and Josie turned to Charity. "I suppose I can't be upset with you, Charity." She sighed. "After all, you probably missed home. But you need to stay at the Carters' house for now. Come on, let's get you back, and I'll have a look at that door. You are a pretty clever horse to break free."

Charity lifted her head from the grass and tossed her mane proudly.

Josie dragged Charity away from the grass and headed back to the Carters'. As they neared the stables, Josie saw Ellie rushing to greet them. The little girl ran straight toward Charity, calling out her name.

"You found her!" she said breathlessly to Josie. "I was bringing her some apples, but when I got to the stall it was empty. I was so worried."

"Well," Josie said, smiling. "I've brought Charity back safe and sound." She looked at Ellie. "And I bet she'd like one of those apples now."

"Really?" Ellie's face broke into a smile and Josie's heart caught in her throat as she saw the delight on the little girl's face.

"I'll put Charity back in her stall, and then you

can give her that treat," she suggested. Ellie nodded, happy to be helping.

When Charity was safely put away, Ellie and Josie fed Charity the apples. Ellie laughed delightedly, watching Charity crunch on the tasty snack.

Mrs. Carter came out of the house and stood next to Josie. "Ellie was so worried about Charity," she said in a confidential whisper. "I think she's so relieved to have her back, she's forgotten to be scared of her! Having Charity here has been the best medicine for Ellie."

Josie was thrilled. "It does look like Ellie is getting used to Charity after all," she agreed, nodding in the direction of the stall where Ellie stood gazing at the gray mare.

"Now we just need to make sure Charity doesn't run away again," Mrs. Carter added with a laugh.

Josie smiled guiltily. "I'm so sorry about that," she said. "I'll have a look at that door and see if I can make it more secure."

She turned to Ellie. "Would you like to hold Charity while I take a look at her stall door?" she asked the little girl.

Ellie took a step back. "That's okay, I'll just

watch you," she said quickly. Mrs. Carter and Josie exchanged knowing glances.

"One step at a time," Mrs. Carter whispered to Josie. "I'll hold Charity," she added in a louder voice. "Ellie, come over next to me."

Ellie nodded and moved beside her mother.

While Mrs. Carter took the lead, Josie inspected the stall door. It was just as she had suspected. The bolt was heavy but large. Easy enough for Charity to get a good grip on with her teeth and pull it back. Josie frowned. "I guess the best solution for now would be to secure the bolt with string," she suggested to Mrs. Carter. "Two devices should be enough to keep her in."

"Why don't you put her in the stall and I'll see if I can find some string in the house?" Mrs. Carter offered.

"Good idea," Josie agreed. As Mrs. Carter went inside, Josie led Charity back into the stall. The horse began munching contentedly on hay while Ellie hung around outside, watching closely.

"Charity's very smart, isn't she?" Ellie said to Josie. "I'm glad she's back."

Josie came out of the stall and stood beside Ellie.

"There was one time when Charity really was lost," she told her.

Ellie was fascinated. "Oh, really? Tell me the story, Josie," she said eagerly. "Please."

"All right," Josie said, laughing. As Ellie settled herself on an upturned barrel, Josie began to tell her of the time Charity was taken from her field by another girl and how she was rescued from a raging river.

Ellie listened intently. "That was a good story," she said as Josie finished. "I'm glad Charity was safe in the end."

"We all were," Josie agreed, sighing at the thought of what could have happened.

Just then Mrs. Carter appeared. "I found some string," she declared.

"Thanks," Josie replied, taking the ball of twine.

Mrs. Carter turned to Ellie. "Come on, Ellie," she said. "Let Josie work on things here. Say good-bye to Charity for now."

Ellie sighed. She walked over to the stable and reached in to give Charity a small pat on the nose. "Will you tell me some more stories about Charity later?" she asked Josie.

"Of course," Josie replied. "Anytime."

As Mrs. Carter led Ellie back inside the house, Josie turned to Charity. "Keep up the good work," she said softly. "Ellie's starting to really like you."

"Will you tell me about Charity's river adventure again, Josie," Ellie begged. She stood fiddling with the string on the stall door, while Josie combed out her horse's white mane.

"Again?" Josie laughed good-naturedly. "I must have told you that story about twenty times by now. Aren't you tired of hearing it?"

"No," Ellie said firmly.

It was a warm afternoon a few days after Charity's escape from the Carters' stables. Josie had secured the bolt firmly with string and the gray mare hadn't managed to find a way out since. The longer Charity stayed, the more Ellie got used to having her around. Now, whenever Josie came to feed Charity, or groom her, or take her out for a ride, Ellie would be there, chatting or handing her the things she needed. Sometimes Josie would arrive at the stable to see Ellie leaning over the door, talking to Charity.

Today, Ellie had come to watch Josie cool Charity down after a particularly long, hot ride. They'd been playing in the twenty-acre field for over an hour. Charity had enjoyed the exercise, but even after a drink she was still warm from her workout.

"Hand me that currycomb, would you, Ellie?" Josie asked her helper. She pointed to the box of grooming tools.

"That's the rubber one, right?" Ellie said.

"Right." Josie smiled. "You're beginning to know everything about horses."

"I'm trying," Ellie said proudly. She turned to reach down for the comb.

As she did so, a large fly began buzzing around Josie's head. Josie batted irritably at the annoying insect. "Go away," she said crossly. Unfortunately, as she swatted, the back of her hand collided with Charity's face. Charity tossed her mane in surprise and took a step backward.

"Look out!" Josie called, as she realized that Ellie was standing right behind Charity.

But it was too late. Charity had stomped on Ellie's toe! Ellie let out a yelp and dropped the currycomb. The noise agitated Charity even more. She took a side step and bumped into Ellie, almost knocking her over. As Josie turned around to check whether Ellie was all right, Mrs. Carter came rushing out of the house to see what all the commotion was about. By that time, Ellie was crying loudly.

"What happened?" gasped Mrs. Carter.

"Charity stamped on my foot!" Ellie managed to blurt out between sobs.

"Calm down," Mrs. Carter said. "Let me take a look."

As Ellie hobbled over to sit on the grass, Josie put a hand on Charity's neck and tried to calm the horse down. Josie felt her begin to relax.

Mrs. Carter undid her daughter's sneaker and slowly peeled back her sock. Sure enough, from where she was standing, Josie could see that Ellie's toes were already beginning to swell.

Ellie clung to her mother. "I don't like Charity anymore!" the little girl cried. Josie was heartbroken. Poor Ellie was back to square one, all because of a silly accident.

"Charity didn't mean to step on you," Josie tried to explain. "She was frightened by the bug. That's why she jumped. She had no clue you were right there, Ellie."

But Ellie just buried her face deeper in her

mother's shoulder. Mrs. Carter picked her daughter up. "I think those toes need some ice on them," she said soothingly. "And we'll ask Dad to look at them when he gets home. You'll be fine, sweetie, don't worry." As she carried her inside, she turned to Josie. "I think we'd better keep these two away from each other for a while," she said.

Josie watched them go, a sinking feeling in her stomach. Charity was now hanging her head as if to say "sorry." "I think we're in trouble, Charity," Josie moaned softly. "Oh, why did I have to hit that silly bug, just when Ellie was beginning to feel safe?" She led Charity back into the stall and gathered up her brush box. After a while, Mrs. Carter came back into the yard.

"How's Ellie?" Josie asked.

Mrs. Carter smiled wearily. "I've put some ice on her toes to reduce the swelling," she said. "Right now she's cuddled up on the sofa watching her favorite movie." Mrs. Carter paused. "But I'm afraid she's still quite upset and nervous about Charity," she went on. "She's been badly hurt by a horse before, and I think this incident has brought all those memories flooding back."

"But this was an accident," Josie assured her. "Charity wouldn't deliberately hurt Ellie."

"I know that, Josie." Mrs. Carter held up her hand to halt Josie's outburst. "I've seen how gentle Charity is. She's a sweetheart. And Ellie had just started to feel comfortable with her. I thought we were really making progress." She sighed heavily. "But I'm afraid this whole incident has really upset Ellie. At the moment she says she won't come outside because Charity is here. I'm sorry, Josie." Mrs. Carter's voice was firm. "I'm going to have to ask you to find another home for Charity. As soon as possible, please."

CHAPTER
NINE

"So that's it," Josie said to Anna. "Charity has to go." The two friends had spent the morning swimming at the town pool and now the bus had dropped them off near Josie's house. "I've got to find another home for her," Josie continued. "Immediately."

"How soon is immediately?" asked Anna.

Josie shrugged and shifted her bag on her shoulder. "Mrs. Carter said as soon as possible," she explained. "Ellie is pretty upset."

"So what are you going to do?" asked Anna. "Where's Charity going to go? What did your mother say?" She fired the questions so quickly at Josie that she held up her hands as if in self-defense.

"Whoa, slow down, Anna," she said, laughing despite herself.

"Sorry," Anna shrugged apologetically. "But this is a crisis, Josie. Something has to be done—for Charity's sake." Josie sighed. Anna was perhaps being melodramatic, but she had a point.

"I know," Josie agreed. "I'm not sure what to do. Mrs. Carter was really nice about it all, but I know she's worried about Ellie," she explained. "Apparently she told my mom that Ellie hadn't adjusted to the move well, and now this business with Charity is stressing her out even more. She just wants Ellie to have a quiet couple of weeks before she starts school." Josie paused and sighed heavily. "I don't know who to feel more sorry for, Ellie or Charity! Ellie thinks it's all her fault that Charity has to go. I know she wants to be friends with her, but she's still so scared."

Anna interrupted. "But Charity is going to be homeless because of a situation that wasn't her fault."

Josie sighed. "It's a lose-lose situation. I said exactly the same thing to my mom," she told Anna. "But she totally understands Mrs. Carter's point of view. She said that if Mrs. Carter wants Charity to leave, then she must. The trouble is, my parents haven't come up with an alternative plan for Charity. Lonsdale is full."

"We'll just have to put our thinking caps on," Anna declared. "We'll find a solution, Josie, I know we will." She linked her arm through her friend's as they walked. "Right after lunch we'll come up with a great plan. Swimming always makes me hungry, and you know I can't think on an empty stomach."

Josie smiled at her friend's determination, but deep down she was worried. What would happen to Charity? Where *would* Charity go?

"Thank you, Mr. Grace, that was delicious." Anna finished her last mouthful of lasagna and put down her fork.

"There's ice cream too, if anyone wants some," Mr. Grace offered. "Josie? Anna?"

"No thanks, Dad," Josie said with a weak smile. "I'm not feeling very hungry today."

Anna opened her mouth and then seemed to think better of it. "Actually, I think I'll pass, too," she said, shooting a sympathetic look at Josie.

"Fair enough," Mr. Grace gathered up the plates and carried them to the sink. "Is everything all right?" he asked when he came back into the dining room. "You seem a little down, Josie. Are you worried about where Charity is going to stay?"

Josie sighed. "Yes," she said. "Anna and I are trying to think of a place for her to go, but we haven't got any ideas yet."

Her dad smiled and sat down at the table again. "There's no need to think of anything," he told her. "We, or rather, your mother, has come up with a solution."

Josie was amazed. Then she had a thought. "It's not Lonsdale, is it?" she asked.

"No, it's not Lonsdale," her dad replied. "They are still booked. No, this place we've found won't cost much, but I'm afraid it is rather far away."

"Come on, Dad, tell us where it is." Josie was getting impatient.

Mr. Grace explained. "Your mother has been talking to the Atterburys, and they agreed to keep Charity in their field until a space is available at Lonsdale." He leaned back in the chair and folded his arms, looking pleased with himself. "See? Problem solved."

"The Atterburys' field." Anna turned to Josie, her eyes shining. "You came up with that idea ages ago. It's not too bad, is it?"

Josie fiddled with her knife and fork. "I do like the idea of Charity being with Faith," she began slowly. She tried hard not to sound too upset, but the thought of not being next to Charity—which was what had bothered her all along—was still stuck firmly in her mind. "It's just so far away. I probably wouldn't be able to see Charity every day. Will it be too much for Jill to have two horses to look after?" she finished.

"Josie, you need to be realistic. No, you won't be able to see as much of Charity," her dad admitted. "But she'll be in a good home, and Mrs. Atterbury has promised to help Jill look after both horses. It won't be forever." Mr. Grace moved around to Josie's seat and put his hand on her shoulder. "I know having Charity next door was the ideal solution for you," he said carefully, "but we'll just have to accept that it didn't work out. Charity will be fine with Jill, I promise."

Josie smiled. "I know, Dad. It's a perfectly reasonable solution. Charity will have a great time with Faith. I'll just have to get used to it."

"Good girl," Mr. Grace was pleased. "All right then, I'm going to wash the dishes." He smiled at the two girls. "Why don't I drive you over to Jill's house later on?" he suggested. "I have to go and pick your mother up in Littlehaven, and it will give you a chance to take some things over and get the place ready."

"That's a great idea, Dad," Josie replied. "Want to come, Anna?"

"I'd love to," replied Anna, "but I can't. I have a haircut this afternoon. Mom's coming to pick me up around two."

"We need to leave around then anyway," said Mr. Grace. "Now, get out of the kitchen so I can clean up."

Josie was quiet for a while as she thought about the new plan. It was true, having Charity next door had been ideal, but it just hadn't worked. She had to admit that keeping her horse at the Atterburys' was a sensible solution, even if it was farther away. Once again Josie felt a little flicker of disappointment that her entire summer wasn't going to be spent with Charity, and, for a brief moment, she felt homesick for School Farm and the stables there. But she quickly pushed this thought to the back of her head. There was nothing she could do about it now and feeling miserable wasn't going to help matters. It was more disappointing that her plan to cure Ellie's fear of horses hadn't worked. She had been looking forward to seeing Ellie and Charity getting along. "Let's go and see Charity," she suggested to Anna. "After all, it's going to get a lot harder to do that."

Anna followed Josie out of the back door and along the path. "At least you know she's going to a good home," she pointed out.

"That's true," Josie agreed, smiling back at her friend.

As they passed Charity's field, Josie looked to see if there had been any progress. It didn't look like it. Big chunks of field were still dug up and there were tools, metal sheets, and plastic tubing everywhere. It was a mess and Josie couldn't imagine that the field would ever be back to normal again.

Charity was waiting for them in her stall, looking out over the door. She nickered softly as they approached, and Josie was pleased to see Ellie back in her usual place on the back steps, not far from the stable. On her lap she held her doll, while Barker scurried about at her feet. When she saw Josie and Anna, she smiled shyly. "Charity looked lonely, so I brought Isabel out to keep her company," she told them.

"That was a good idea," Josie said gently.

Ellie turned to her now, with an anxious look. "Do you think Charity is mad at me, Josie?" she asked.

Josie shook her head. "Not at all, Ellie," she reassured the little girl. "Why do you say that?"

Ellie shrugged her shoulders and looked down at the ground. "Because she can't stay here. I don't really want her to go away," she added in a small voice. "But sometimes I just can't help being afraid of her."

Josie walked over to the steps and crouched down beside her. "You'll make friends with her in time, Ellie. I'm sure you will," she said softly. "You're a very brave girl."

Ellie gave a doubtful smile. "Really?" she asked.

"Absolutely," Josie said, firmly. "You came out here

all by yourself, didn't you, to keep an eye on Charity?"

"Well, I did have Isabel with me," Ellie told her.

"Then Isabel's brave, too." Josie straightened up. "Look, I've brought Charity some treats. Would you like to help me feed her?"

"No thanks," Ellie said quickly. "I'd rather just watch you, if that's all right."

"Of course," Josie smiled. She tried not to be disappointed that Ellie didn't want to help.

She exchanged a quick glance with Anna, who gave her an encouraging thumbs-up sign. Then she reached into her pocket for the treats and held them out to Charity, who grabbed them greedily. Anna reached around to pat Charity on the neck and the horse, thinking she had some more food, nibbled at her shoulder playfully.

"Ugh. Charity just gave me a sloppy kiss!" Anna exclaimed, wiping horse drool from her shoulder.

Ellie began to laugh. It was clear that she was enjoying watching. But by the time Josie and Anna had to go, she still hadn't moved any closer to Charity. She stayed watching from the step, keeping a tight hold on Isabel. Josie looked at her thoughtfully. If only she could find a way to conquer

106

Ellie's fear. She needed more time. But Charity was leaving soon. Time was the one thing they just didn't have.

Later that afternoon, Mr. Grace dropped Josie off at Jill Atterbury's house. "I'll be back in about an hour to pick you up," he told her.

"I know how frustrating this must be for you, Josie," Jill said after he had gone. "But don't worry, we'll take good care of Charity." They were in Jill's room. Josie sat at the end of Jill's bed, looking around at the horse posters plastering the walls.

"I know you will, Jill," she said with a smile. "Charity will do fine with you and Faith. I just wish you lived closer."

"Yes, sorry about that," Jill said sympathetically. "It is too bad that the stable next door didn't work out."

Josie sighed. "Ellie just had a bad scare. Now she can't trust any horse, not even one as gentle as Charity."

Jill walked over to her window and gazed out over the field. "I think I might know how she feels," she began slowly.

Josie was curious. "What are you talking about? You've never been hurt by a horse," she said.

"No," Jill replied. "But when I started riding Faith after my accident, I was still scared of being hurt again. And what if I fell off Faith? What if I had an accident when I was riding her? I didn't want to go through that again." Jill sighed and sat down on the bed beside Josie.

"So what happened?" Josie was fascinated.

Jill looked down at her hands. "I think I got fed up with being afraid," she explained quietly. "I just wanted to get on with my life. So I took the risk, and I'm glad I did. Riding Faith means more to me than anything, and I'm not scared anymore."

Josie thought about what Jill had said for a moment. Then she leaped off the bed excitedly. "You know, Jill, you've just given me the best idea!" she exclaimed.

"I can see that." Jill laughed. "So, what is it?"

Josie turned to Jill. "Ellie loves hearing stories about the people and horses I know," she explained quickly. "Hearing your story could be just what she needs. It's got to be worth a try."

Jill was pleased. "Well, I like the idea of being an

inspiration to someone," she admitted. "But do you really think my story will make a difference to Ellie?"

"I do, Jill. I think it just might mean *all* the difference," Josie declared firmly.

All the way home in the car Josie thought about Jill's story. She was sure that once Ellie heard it, she would not be scared anymore. And if Josie was honest with herself, she was also hoping that Ellie would want Charity to stay.

"You're very quiet in the back, there, Josie," Mr. Grace commented from the driver's seat.

"Just thinking about things, Dad," Josie replied. "Do you mind dropping me off at the Carters' house? I want to go and check on Charity."

As soon as the car stopped, Josie jumped out and ran up to the Carters' front door. She wanted to tell Ellie about Jill. But when she rounded the corner she saw that Jill's story would have to wait. Ellie was pacing up and down, sobbing.

"What's the matter?" Josie asked as soon as she saw the little girl's face streaked with tears.

Ellie turned to her in dismay. "It's Isabel," she cried. "I can't find her and I've looked everywhere. Do you think she's run away like Charity did?"

Josie gave Ellie a big hug. "Don't worry. I'll help you look for her," she offered. "I'm sure she must be around here somewhere."

"Thanks, Josie," Ellie said, trying to swallow her sobs. "I just have to find her."

Josie and Ellie began to search the yard. But it was a big place and although they searched for a long time, there was still no sign of the doll.

Mrs. Carter came walking across the lawn toward them. "I can't find her in the house, darling," she called to Ellie.

"Josie's been helping me look outside, but we can't find her here, either," Ellie wailed.

Mrs. Carter smiled gratefully at Josie. "Thanks for the help," she said. "It's very nice of you." She turned to Ellie again. "Why don't you come inside and have some dinner?" she suggested gently. "We can look again before bedtime."

"No. I have to find Isabel," Ellie protested.

Josie knelt down in front of her. "Go and have dinner now, Ellie," she said. "I'll come back later and help you look for Isabel. We'll find her, I promise."

Ellie agreed reluctantly and slowly followed her mother indoors. Josie watched them go. She hated to see Ellie so sad. She knew that Isabel helped Ellie not to feel homesick for her old house and friends—and Josie knew all about feeling homesick. Plus, the sooner she found Isabel, the sooner Ellie could hear Jill's story.

CHAPTER TEN

Josie looked at her watch impatiently. Ellie must have finished dinner by now. There wasn't much light left and she still hadn't told Ellie Jill's story. "That will have to wait, I suppose, Basil," she said, scratching the little terrier's back. "First I have to find Isabel. I wonder if she's turned up yet?"

Basil chewed on his rubber ball.

"I can see you're not interested at all," Josie said, laughing at him. "But I've got a job to do."

Josie opened the back door and slipped outside. "Take your jacket with you if you're going out," her mother called, but Josie was already halfway down the path. The evening was still warm, and Josie felt comfortable in her T-shirt. She gathered her auburn hair into a ponytail and lifted it from her neck, enjoying the feel of the breeze on her skin.

At the Carters' house Josie bumped into Mrs. Carter coming out of the front door. "I don't understand where Ellie could have left that doll," she said. "We've turned the house upside down and searched the yard, too. She'll be inconsolable if it's lost."

"I've come back to help," Josie said. "I'll take one more look in the yard."

"Why not?" Mrs. Carter agreed. "It can't do any harm. Thank you so much, Josie. You've been great. I'm sorry things didn't work out with you keeping Charity here."

Josie's heart sank as she followed Mrs. Carter around to the back garden. She knew Charity had to go, but hearing Mrs. Carter say it again only made it sound more final. "I understand," she managed to say. "But I still hope Ellie and Charity can be friends one day."

"So do I," Mrs. Carter smiled down at her. "Now, where is Ellie?" She suddenly slowed, staring across the yard, and Josie followed her gaze. A strange sight greeted her. For a few moments, Josie could do nothing but watch in amazement. Charity was walking calmly across the lawn, heading straight for the hedge that bordered her own field and the back of the Carters' garden.

"How on earth—?" Mrs. Carter began.

"Oh no," Josie groaned. "Charity must have undone the string I tied around the bolt. She's trickier than I thought!"

"She certainly seems determined to escape," Mrs. Carter agreed. "Maybe she's telling us she wants to go home."

Josie moved toward her horse. "I'll go and catch her," she said quickly.

"No, wait." Mrs. Carter put a hand on Josie's arm. "Look."

Josie stopped and looked where Mrs. Carter was pointing. To her surprise she saw Ellie, standing at the edge of the lawn, watching the horse intently. Josie and Mrs. Carter hung back, waiting to see what would happen. Ellie waited, too. Charity reached the hedge and pushed her nose into the bushes. She's probably munching on something tasty, Josie thought.

Suddenly she saw a huge grin spread across Ellie's face. "Of course, my spy hole," Josie heard her say. "Now I remember! Clever Charity."

To Josie's astonishment, Ellie walked straight toward Charity. The horse took a small side step away—as if sensing that the little girl was wary of her. But Ellie didn't appear worried in the slightest. Instead, she reached into the bushes, near the very spot Charity had been nosing around. When she pulled her hand out again, Josie was surprised to see her holding Isabel. Ellie turned to Charity triumphantly. "You found Isabel for me, Charity. Thank you."

As Josie and Mrs. Carter started across the lawn, Ellie held out her hand and cautiously gave Charity a pat on the nose.

Mrs. Carter whispered excitedly to Josie, "I think Ellie just got over her fear."

As Josie caught up with Charity and put a hand on her neck, Ellie turned, her eyes wide with excitement.

"I was playing hide-and-seek with Isabel by the spy hole," she explained excitedly. "I forgot I'd hidden her there. But somehow Charity knew. And she escaped from her stall just to help me find her. I'm sure of it!" Suddenly, Ellie turned and flung her arms around Charity's neck. "You're a clever, clever horse," she cried. And Josie, reaching up to stroke Charity's mane, couldn't have agreed more.

"So Charity stood there looking very pleased with herself, while Ellie rescued her doll from the bush," Josie told Anna, as she tightened Charity's girth. "And then Ellie gave Charity a big hug."

Anna gave Charity a congratulatory pat on the neck. "Well done, little girl," she said. "So what happened next?"

"Well, Charity was everybody's hero, especially Ellie's!" Josie said.

Josie was filling Anna in on all the details as she tacked Charity up. "Ellie's convinced Charity deliberately found Isabel for her. She's really happy to have the doll back. And now she and Charity are the best of friends!" Josie explained happily.

"So Charity's an escape artist and a doll detective!" Anna said, laughing.

"It certainly looks like it," Josie agreed. "But you want to know the best part?"

"Mrs. Carter said Charity can stay?" Anna guessed.

Josie nodded her head happily. "Exactly. For as long as she needs to."

"That's great—as long as she doesn't escape again," Anna pointed out with a laugh.

Josie groaned. "Don't even joke about it," she warned. "Charity only got away with it last time because she found the doll and got on Ellie's good side." She turned to the gray mare and looked seriously into her big, brown eyes. "I won't be pleased with you if you try this stunt again, young lady," she said sternly.

"You wouldn't dare, would you, Charity?" Anna tickled her nose. "So does Jill mind that Charity won't be coming to stay with her?"

Josie shook her head. "Not at all," she replied. "I'd already told her about Ellie and how scared she was of Charity. Jill's just happy that everything worked out so well for us in the end."

"Well, Charity certainly is comfortable here," Anna commented. "Now who gets to ride first today?" she asked. "You or me?"

"Me," a small voice announced proudly. The two friends looked down to see Ellie standing there dressed in brand-new britches and a riding hat. Anna turned openmouthed to Josie, who was also looking down at Ellie in amazement.

"Of course, you can ride Charity," Josie said. "But are you sure you want to?"

Just then Mrs. Carter appeared. "If it's all right with you, Josie," she said. "Ellie's been asking and asking if she can ride Charity. With you leading, of course."

"Mom's going to let me start riding lessons at Lonsdale," Ellie declared happily.

"That's fantastic." Josie was thrilled. "They have some beautiful horses there, Ellie."

"Not as beautiful as Charity, though," Ellie ran a hand along the horse's mane. "I know Charity can't stay here forever, but she'll always be my friend, won't she?"

Josie looked at Ellie. She couldn't believe how relaxed she was with Charity now. "Of course she will. And you'll be able to visit her any time you like, Ellie. You don't even have to ask."

Ellie smiled delightedly. "Maybe I'll even have a horse of my own one day," she said. "After all, I've got the perfect stables!"

Mrs. Carter raised her hand to slow Ellie down. "One thing at a time, Ellie," she said, laughing. "It's hard work looking after a horse."

Josie grinned too. Now she only hoped that nothing would happen to spoil Ellie's first ride. After all that had gone on, Josie was almost too frightened to try. But one look at Ellie's excited face told her she had. And there was only one way to find out. If Ellie was ready, then she had to trust that Charity was too.

"I'll adjust the stirrups and then I'll help you mount," Josie suggested. Her fingers were trembling with nervous excitement as she got Charity ready. Once she was sure that things were all in place, Josie handed the reins to Ellie. "Are you ready?" she asked her.

"Yup!" said the little girl brightly.

"I'll give you a leg up," Mrs. Carter said. She hooked her hands together and helped Ellie to swing up into the saddle.

Josie held her breath. Beside her she sensed that Mrs. Carter was nervous too and Anna was watching in anxious silence. Only Ellie seemed relaxed as she settled herself into the saddle, slotting her feet easily into the stirrups, as if she had been doing this her whole life.

"Please stand still, Charity," Josie murmured under her breath as she stroked the gray mare's neck, willing her to stay calm. But she didn't need to worry. As if she understood the situation exactly, Charity stood perfectly still. Josie held on to her bridle and gave the horse a grateful pat. "How does it feel up there?" she asked Ellie.

"Great!" Ellie replied, grinning from ear to ear.

"Not too high?" Mrs. Carter asked anxiously.

"No, Charity's perfect," Ellie told her confidently.

Josie let out the breath she had been holding. "In that case, let's walk on," she said, smiling. Everything was going to be all right.

THE
HORSESHOE
TRILOGIES

Don't miss the first three heartwarming horse stories . . .

BOOK ONE:
Keeping Faith

BOOK TWO:
Last Hope

BOOK THREE:
Sweet Charity

Josie Grace has grown up with three beloved horses—Faith, Hope, and Charity—at her mother's riding school. But when the stables are forced to close, the family must find the animals new homes. While Josie is devastated at first, her personal mission to match Faith, Hope, and Charity with the perfect owners allows her to form a new, special bond with her favorite mares.

VOLO Available now in your local bookstore.
Visit us at www.volobooks.com